From
ANN MARGRET
To
BATTLE STATIONS

Life Aboard A Carrier
in Viet Nam

Don Horne

HORNE PUBLISHING

RED OAK, TEXAS

FROM

ANN MARGRET

TO

BATTLE STATIONS

Copyright © 2010 by Don Horne

ISBN-13: 978-0615432816

ISBN-10: 0615432816

Printed in USA by Create Space

(www.createspace.com)

Horne Publishing

302 Cascade Drive

Red Oak, Texas 75154

Dedication

This story is dedicated to all the veterans that went to war as a young man and came back an old man in just 4 years or less. We went away as kids and came back as warriors.

I had a hard time relating to my friends who wrote me telling about pep rallies, football games, and campus activities while I was loading bombs on aircraft and worrying about making it back in one piece. Still, we were young and we had friends closer than our siblings. The shared experiences, which this book is about, are the only reason we can look back and wish we could do it all over again.

*P*reface

The most horrific aspect of war to me is thinking of a young man engaged in a fight for his life when only a few weeks before he was chasing girls or a degree in some ivy covered college. Especially when they don't come back.

I did not <u>mean</u> to go to war. I thought I wanted to run away to have a life of my own, and to get away from an over controlling father. My idea when the whole thing started was to see exotic ports of call while in the company of good friends, and we all had on the same uniform. My time in the Navy did include some exotic parts of call, but not the European cruise I actually had in mind. However, like most young men who spent their late teens and early twenties in the military, I would not take anything for the memories.

Chapter One

In early August of 1963, my friends, Jerry and John, and I were sitting in the back of John's pickup cooling down after a hot night game of softball. We finished off our Cokes, and I would not let the guys break the bottles because we could get three cents each for them. School was getting ready to start and we all three went to different colleges. I was having a little problem deciding what I really wanted to study. In only 2 semesters I had changed my major twice. I told the guys I had been thinking about going to the Navy. They were perfectly happy staying in Alabama, but whatever was out there for me was just that...out there.

"You know," began Jerry, "I am still thirsty. We should have gotten another drink before the filling station closed."

"I agree," said John, "But do you know what would really taste good is a ripe watermelon."

Jerry and I both agreed, and just like that we began to form the plan to go on a crime spree. We knew that Mr. Oaks had the largest patch of the biggest, best tasting watermelons around. We figured if we slipped into his patch and "borrowed" a couple that he would never miss them.

We were giggling together just imagining what a double handful of a big, juicy, red-meated black diamond watermelon would taste like. We looked at each other, and John got out of the back and started the truck while Jerry and I sat in the back where it was cool. We did not have to ask, for we knew where we were going.

We cruised quietly through downtown Vincent, out the highway, and turned off onto the dirt road leading to Mr. Oak's farm. The road was curvy and hilly and a half mile or so before the farm John cut the lights and the starlight and the light from a half moon were all the light we needed to guide us to the scene of the crime.

Mr. Oak's huge melon patch grew right up to the edge of the road, and we just walked out a few feet and all of us pulled a couple of huge watermelons. We had one under each arm as we started walking back up the road toward the truck.

All of a sudden, we heard Mr. Oak's two hound dogs commence to set up a racket. Even though we knew they were in a pen, we took off running like they were on our heels. Jerry beat us to the truck, took our watermelons and put them into the bed while John started the truck.. I vaulted over the side as he put the truck in reverse and quickly turned around. Even with not much light, we could see the road well enough to drive away far enough to turn on the lights without having to worry about being seen.

As the lights lit up the road, we started laughing and yelling believing we had gotten away. We drove for about fifteen minutes to a roadside park. There we each took our purloined melons, threw them to the ground to split them open, and then thrust our hands into the hearts of the melons to grasp huge, dripping handfuls of red, water filled mounds of ecstasy!

We savagely ripped and snorted and devoured the melons all the way to the light green rinds. They were the best watermelons we had ever had. We looked like wild animals to one another with the red juice dripping from our chins, like blood, and all over our shirts and jeans. We put our faces right into the open melons without worrying about getting messy! My impression of that night we were like three wolves, or some other kind of wild predator, devouring our kill! In only a few minutes we took the rinds, put them into the big trash barrels, and took off our shirts and washed them under the water faucet at the park. Our shirts already were wet from sweat, and putting them back on was a cool sensation for the ride back to town. By the time John dropped us off at our homes our shirts were almost dry, and the only evidence of our crime was a few drops on our jeans.

I undressed in the laundry room and put my clothes in the washer. I then sneaked through the house in my underwear to the bathroom where I took a quick bath and dried off. Once in my bedroom and in bed, I can remember fluffing my pillow somewhat, and my next conscious thought was how good Mom's bacon and coffee smelled. I told my mom I was just tired, and truthfully I was, and that is why I was so quiet at the breakfast table. I ate, put on a clean t-shirt, and started mowing the yard like a fiend. The hard work seemed to help my feeling of guilt we had done something we should not have. Mr. Oaks went to the same church as us, and was even a good friend of my dad's! The guilt was eating at me!

Just after lunch, I borrowed the car and went all the way out to Mr. Oak's house. It was a well-kept wooden house with a big front porch. Of course he was sitting out on his front porch, and I hoped he would not have me arrested. I got out of the car resigned to my fate.

"Hey, Don!" said Mr. Oaks with a smile. That did not help my feelings at all for him to be so friendly. "Come on up and sit for a spell!"

"Mr. Oaks," I started. "I came last night and swiped a couple of melons and if you will tell me how much I owe you, I will make it right. I promise to never do it again!"

I had my head down looking at my feet feeling as low as I could possibly feel for him to know I was a thief. When I looked up he was smiling!

"You know, Don, I have over 2 acres in ripe watermelons and I meant to tell you, Jerry and John to come help yourselves."

"Well, I guess we did, didn't we? But I apologize for doing it in the middle of the night, Mr. Oaks."

He got up and came to where I was standing and hugged me.

"Although I didn't know about it. I don't care one little bit. You don't owe me anything, son."

With tears in my eyes, I asked, "Will you forgive me? I just don't have the heart to do that sort of thing."

He patted my shoulder and laughed, "I am impressed you would come and confess and offer to pay. It took a man to do that and I appreciate it. But, there's nothing to forgive."

He looked over my shoulder, smiled, and spoke to me softly and said, "Here comes John and Jerry! Let's have a little fun."

He turned on his heel quickly, opened the screen door and went inside. John drove the truck up close to the steps, and he and Jerry got out.

"Was he mad?" queried Jerry.

"I don't know yet. He went in the house as soon as he saw you two coming!"

Just at that moment Mr. Oaks slammed open the screen door and stood there with his long barreled shotgun in his hand and frowning!

By then I had caught on to what he was up to, and I was choking on my tongue to keep from laughing out loud at Jerry and John as they raised their hands as if they expected to be shot at any moment!

"Well now wait a minute, Mr. Oaks. I confess we all took 2 melons a piece, but we are here to tell you and make it right! Please don't shoot us!" Jerry said with a quivering lower lip.

My friend, John, when scared, like when we went to see the scary movie, Psycho, his sinuses would run. He started sniffing like a bloodhound on a trail.

"Please, Mr. Oaks! Sniff. We are so sorry. Sniff. If you will let us pay you for the melons, we will never set foot on your property again! Sniff."

I was still standing beside Mr. Oaks on the porch looking down at my frightened friends. He did not point the gun at them at all, but he did not even crack a smile as he scowled down at them and said, "Well, what if I WANT you to come back? You don't ever visit me except in the dead of night. How about coming around when you see ripe melons and saying hello at least! You can have all you want for free!"

He started laughing so uproariously he had tears in his eyes.

"Boys, I would never shoot you! I was just funning! This gun ain't even loaded!"

So, the tension in the air cleared, and although I laughed, Jerry and John just giggled a little. They were still a little wary.

Mr. Oaks invited them up on the porch and found seats for all of us while he went inside again and brought out watermelon and lemonade. It took a few minutes to become comfortable, but we figured we deserved to let Mr. Oaks have a good laugh at our expense after stealing his melons. However, that is the only time in my life the taste of watermelon almost made me throw up!

Later, he hugged all three of us and picked out two huge melons for each of us as we made ready to leave. As we loaded the melons in my car and John's pickup, Mr. Oaks said almost sadly, "I know all you kids, and, the truth is, I really <u>would</u> enjoy a visit once in a while. Don't be a stranger!"

We drove off waving after promising to come again soon, but we all three agreed it would be in daylight!

The next day was Sunday, and Mom and Dad invited Mr. Oaks home with us to eat lunch. She had fried chicken, mashed potatoes with all the trimmings, and had even baked a cake to go with the fresh watermelon I had brought home. For once, I passed on the melon and just ate cake!

Chapter Two

"I don't think so, son," I heard my daddy say. "If I let you buy that car you will start running up and down the road, racing, and eventually wrap yourself around a tree."

I had asked my dad to let me buy a 1950 Ford that was in primer but had a new interior already finished for only 50 dollars. Flathead engines were very cheap, and I figured I could have a very cool car for under 200 dollars.

My dad was very strict. He was a deacon in a Baptist Church, and he was not abusive to beat us but he had his own ideas of behavior, dress, conversation, etc. Unfortunately for my sister, my brother, and me he was just about 20 years behind the times. I loved him dearly, but he had no clue who we were.

"I love you, Daddy," I said. "But you don't even know who I am. You want to control me and you don't know that you don't have to. I am nearly 19, just finished my second year of college, I am home when I say I will be, and I don't smoke or drink. I just love cars. We missed the restored '40 Ford convertible because you said it was too old. We didn't buy the 55 Pontiac we put the u-joints in because you said 300 dollars was too much. All my friends have cars. What are you punishing me for?"

"I am not punishing you. I just don't want you to wind up in jail like some of your cousins, and as long as you are under my roof you will do as I say."

"That's fair enough. I will call Jerry to take me to Birmingham to the bus station, and I will go to Grandmas' house and go into the Service."

When Jerry came, I saluted my tearful mom, waved good bye to my dad who just looked away, and I took the bus from Birmingham, Alabama, to Russellville, Arkansas, to join the Navy. I visited with my grandparents for a few days before I went to inquire about going into the military.

I actually thought I wanted to join the Air Force when I went to the recruiting office, but this "swabbie", resplendent in his dress whites, asked me, "Why?" He was leaning against the door post of the recruiter's office all lean in his flared pants and his round white hat massaged into a 4 way square. He had a coffee cup in his hand that said, "USS Forrestal." I thought he looked way cool!

With no real reason I could think of to answer him, I said that I wanted to go to electronics school because I already had a couple years of college. He lied and told me the Navy had better schools than the Air Force. So, I took the offered bus ride to Little Rock as a recruit for the United States Navy.

In Little Rock the recruiting office put several of us up for the night at the YMCA. No hotel. I now see why there are homeless people under a bridge instead of the YMCA. I listened to a room full of people snore, I slept on my billfold, and I was <u>not</u> taking off my clothes in front of these people! It was at least a bed.

The next morning, we were fed stale doughnuts and coffee-colored hot water. They took us all to the courthouse, signed us in, swore us in, and because I had had some college, they handed me several sealed, official looking, manila envelopes, and told me to keep up with them and turn them in to the people in San Diego, California, at the Naval Training Center.

I was excited to take my first airplane ride. I was with two other guys from Little Rock going to the Navy, and we left about 6 p.m. in the afternoon. As we loaded, I quickly got to a window seat and beat my companions. After we took off, I was amazed, like a little kid at his first circus, to look out and see the world from that height. It was a panorama of a patchwork quilt of different shades of brown and green.

We got to sit in first class courtesy of the airline, and I was embarrassed to watch my two friends across the aisle arm wrestle trying to impress a cute young thing traveling with who I figured out was a "sugar daddy." The girl's careless, off hand attitude made me guess she might not have had money, but she had been raised around it. She was used to people jumping when she said jump.

Of course she was blonde, as if that really means anything. She was perfectly dressed in a skin tight, form fitting, blue and white dress. She had a small confrontation with the stewardess because she was too young to drink. So, the stewardess sold the older guy two drinks and walked off. Of course, she drank one of them.

They held hands and played cutesie with her rubbing her bare foot against his leg after taking off one of her sandals. I was sitting across from her in a four person face to face arrangement. She smiled a little half smile every time our eyes met. She had the same look a mature woman has who knows her way around men even though she was only eighteen. It was as if she could peer into your heart and soul to see if you were worth the trouble of manipulating.

The woman on my left excused herself to go to the restroom. The girl's older friend got up also to go somewhere, and I went back to looking out the window. By now it was dark, and I was enthralled by the city lights far below. All of a sudden I felt a foot rubbing the inside of my calf! To this day I can remember the sideways smile and the big blue eyes as she said, "You are not going to try to impress me?"

"You keep rubbing that foot against me and I am going to impress you!"

She laughed out loud, and I got an early lesson in flirting with someone I could never have.

When her friend came back she went back to riding with her foot against his calf, but she kept smiling a little smile at me in the semi darkness every time our eyes made contact as he went to sleep.

In the press of bodies as we got off the plane in San Diego, somehow she was behind me. She pressed against me softly, rubbing her hands over me in the semi-darkness, and whispered, "You must work out!"

"College football," I whispered over my shoulder.

"Hmm," she whispered. She kept pressing against me until almost to the exit doorway.

"Bye!" was all she said, gave me a little pat, and then took her friend's hand to go down the steps.

I was still watching her walk away as I stood and waited for my friends. She managed one last backward glance and smile, as I smiled at her and shook my head.

"Welcome to California, Don," laughed Phil Owens, one of the guys who happened to have seen the whole scene.

"You got that right! We are no longer in Kansas, Toto!" We both laughed as I took a deep breath and sighed.

We had landed in San Diego early in the morning after flying from Little Rock all night. I called the number on our order packet, and a big, gray bus with a sleepy E-3 as a driver came and drove us to the Naval Air Station in San Diego. I slept a few fitful minutes on the bus, but was looking forward to a bed. It was 4:30 a.m. when the bus doors opened, and the driver said loudly, "Everyone out!"

Once out of the bus, a big, khaki-clad Chief Petty Officer was yelling for us to "FALL IN" on these little white numbered circles. I did not ask fall into what. I was wise enough to figure out on my own what he wanted. After they had enough circles filled they took us and fed us and I ate well.

My first day in the Navy is a blur as we got outfitted with uniforms, a medical exam, and a haircut. My hair was already in a short flat top and I did not notice much change, but the first man they took was a kid from Chicago that had a thick head of dark black hair combed back on the sides with a little curl hanging down in front. The barber with a friendly smile asked him to be first. He climbed up in the barber's chair and when the barber asked him how he wanted it he said, "Just a trim. I got it cut just before I left home."

"No problem," smiled the barber and two big guys moved a step closer to the man in the chair. The barber took the electric shears and started at the man's forehead and cut a 2 inch wide swath down the middle of all the man's beautiful, thick hair!

"WHAT ARE YOU DOING?" the man yelled.

The men were there for a reason as they had to restrain him to cut all of his hair to match.

The barber then explained that everyone received the same haircut...short.

By the time we had drawn uniforms, changed into them, bundled up and sent home our bags, ate two more times, we went to the barracks. I was asleep on my bunk by 7 p.m. I slept almost until 5 a.m. the next morning. I took a shower, dressed and fell in with my sea bag. I felt rested and ready to go.

In the first few days we moved into our own barracks, and except for everyone yelling at us, I made it okay. They drilled us in marching, and exercised us. I was in shape to go back to school and play football, and the exercising did not bother me. San Diego in September can be hot though. We had a couple guys have some problems marching on the hot asphalt. It was not unusual for one or two to fall out and throw up.

I had had some college and I was made a squad leader and put in the front of a row of men. However, my "three row stride" from being from the farm was not in step with the precision steps our company commander desired. I was treated like Gomer Pyle for a day or two until I learned to shorten my stride. Finally, <u>my</u> squad could stay in step with the company!

We marched several hours a day at first, and our march took us all over the Naval Air Station to learn where every thing was. The training center had a mock up of a ship and we would stop and the company commander would point out the bow, the stern, gangplank, and explain that left was "port" and right was "starboard." We learned what a bulkhead and a hatch were on a ship. One did not "mop the floor" we "swabbed the deck."

About the second week in boot camp, we were stopped by a friend of our company commander, or what might have been a competitor, a company commander of another company. He would grill us and we had to shout back the answer in unison. With nothing else to read on our downtime, I actually read the US

Navy Handbook they issued all of us. One of the questions we were asked was, "What is the length of a double time step?"

I had just read the answer the night before.

"SIR!" I shouted. "THE LENGTH OF A DOUBLE TIME STEP IS 30 INCHES, SIR!"

Of course, the whole company who had not known the answer, joined in unison as we shouted it back to the rival company commander. I saw my company commander smile a little proud smile and turn away. He did not want us to see him. It was the first time we had ever seen him smile!

The disappointed rival commander said glumly, "Very good. Carry on!" He went off marching his company at double time!

About the 4th or 5th week of marching, classes, lectures, etc. we went to a day of shipboard firefighting. They lined us up along a 6 inch water hose and warned us to not let go because of the tremendous pressure. The Chief that was lecturing us had just told the guy holding the hose with his hand on the valve to NOT pull it back until he got out of the way. Yes, you got it right. This guy was not our brightest recruit, and when he pulled back on the valve, the water pressure pinned the screaming Chief against the wall of the building! We all were laughing so hard we could not catch our breath, and I grabbed the hose away from him and turned it off. They sent the guy back to the barracks, he went before a board that afternoon, and we arrived just in time to see him packing his bags. He got a medical discharge. It was warranted, I suppose, but it was still sad to see him in tears.

We had a week of different athletic events, and we won a few races and stuff, but the best for me was the flag football games! I was the quarter-back and we had several fleet of foot guys that had played football before. We won three games by a large margin, and when we got our star patch, we got to sew it on our company flag.

We were the best in our group and on graduation day we got to march first in line. By then I was the APO 1. I was second in command of our company and we made the E-6 First Class Petty Officer Company Commander proud. In fact he made Chief shortly thereafter.

We were put on buses to go to the airport, and there were lots of glad handshakes all around. I flew standby out of San Diego. My folks met me at the airport in Birmingham, Alabama, and my dad, bless his heart, cried as he hugged me. You would have thought I had returned from the war!

Chapter Three

After ten days at home, I rode the bus to Millington, Tennessee, home of the Naval Air Training Station. It was just a few miles from Memphis, Tennessee. Millington is the home of the training school for technical fields, and I was entered in A school for Aviation Electronics Technician. I was given a friendly welcome and a schedule of when to report fully dressed for roll call. For a few days the morning fall out and answer "here" when my name was called was all I did.

After about a week the Chief in charge of my barracks called me in and asked if I wanted to go on temporary duty for 6 weeks while I awaited my school assignment to open up. Best thing I did in the Navy. For 6 weeks, and it wound up being 8, all I did after roll call was sweep, swab, and once a week (usually on Friday) wax one long passageway or hallway. Even working very slowly and diligently, I was usually through by 0900. I would then go to the gym and work out with weights or play sports with the other guys until time for lunch. We were always at the head of the line for chow. It was how I met Joe Belski.

Joe was from Chicago, and had been caught running numbers for the mob as a teenager so many times he was finally given his choice of going to jail or going to the military. When I asked if he had any trouble choosing, he just laughed.

Joe Belski and I had absolutely nothing in common except girls and good times. He smoked, I didn't. He cursed often, I didn't. Even Santa Claus and the sunrise to him had an adjective that ended in ....ing. He was hump shouldered somewhat, sunken chest, and not physically intimidating at all to look at. He was still the strongest man I ever met when it came to arm wrestling.

He was mildly famous in some of the places we went for holding a wrestling antagonist perfectly still with one hand, taking a draw from a cigarette, and pressing him down as if it were nothing. He humbled many guys who just thought they were strong. He claimed it was mostly technique, but whatever it was worked for him.

Belski also could do something well or

better, than any other man I ever met could do...pick up girls. He was the best at it I ever saw. When we went to a club or even just a busy bar, I would find us a booth or a table and he would go off for a few minutes by himself. In just a little while here he would come with the two prettiest girls in the place one on each arm. Whatever mojo or magic he had, the girls loved him. My own mother loved him.

My other best friend in Memphis was Dick Vachon, a muscular, crew cut young man from Massachusetts. Dick started out making fun of my Southern drawl, but he never disrespected me. I explained to him that <u>he</u> was the one with an accent. In the South everyone had the same accent as me. My mother and sister loved him as much as Joe Belski. My mother even told him to come back when he got out of the Navy and she would adopt him. Plus, my sister would have married him. She had good taste, but bad timing. The Navy in a few months would separate all three of us.

I had bought a clean, blue and white 1957 Pontiac 2 door hardtop. We went back and forth to Alabama nearly every weekend, and during the week we all three chased girls with it. It had two bench seats, and three couples were very comfortable riding in it.

I was the driver because it was my car, and because I didn't drink and drive. Since we were going home, I definitely did not want my dad or mom smelling beer on my breath and I would not have been drinking anyway.

The drinking age was 18 in Mississippi and as we went home we would stop at the first package store over the state line and each of the guys would buy a 6 pack apiece. Shortly after finishing off the beer, they, of course, went to sleep and I listened to WLS out of Chicago on the radio. I had a rear seat speaker and a little volume and wind noise would help drown out the two snoring. I considered it ecstasy to drive along late at night with all the windows down on the hardtop listening to rock and roll music. The only time I stopped usually was when someone had to go to the bathroom or for gas.

Once we decided to take another route from Memphis down through central Mississippi across to Birmingham which I had seen on the map. We stopped in a little joint called the Brass Rail around Jackson, Mississippi, about 10 p.m. They had a live band and the large crowd was mostly young.

We went in and the guys ordered beers and I had a Coke. Belski got up and asked a pretty brunette in short shorts that was sitting alone if she would like to dance. She smiled, gave him her hand, and they danced very well together. Belski, being from the big city of Chicago, was an excellent dancer and knew all the coolest moves. With his northern accent he was an instant hit. After a few dances the girls were waiting to dance with him.

After a few minutes of watching Belski, a drunk redneck with a soiled cowboy hat and missing a front tooth came over while Belski was taking a break sitting between a couple of the girls. He put both hands on the table, leaned over, and got to almost touching noses close with Belski and said loudly, "I heard people from up north are gay!"

You could have heard the proverbial pin drop. Belski shrugged and said, "Why, you looking for a date?" Belski smiled and winked at the giggling girls and said, "I'm not gay, but I <u>will</u> sign your dance card if you want me to." The crowd, which was mixed with several military personnel as well as locals, roared.

The redneck blinked in his drunken stupor while he tried to think of something a little more clever to say. When he couldn't he straightened up just a little to throw a punch. Big mistake. Belski threw one punch from just shoulder level and hit the drunk redneck right on the jaw. The redneck went backward and laid out on the floor. He was out cold. We figured it was time to leave and not push our luck. However, when we went to pay, the owner of the bar would not take our money. He was ex-Navy.

"On the house, guys. But you better make tracks. His name is Bubba, and he does not have many friends, but he has a couple of big, mean brothers that just love to finish what Bubba starts!"

In less than 15 seconds, we had kissed the girls, grabbed our drinks, piled into the car, and slung just a little gravel getting out of the parking lot. We never took that route again to go to Birmingham from Memphis.

Within a couple of months Dick went to Aviation Metalsmith school in Norfolk, and Joe Belski and I graduated from A school. Joe went on to the West Coast while I stayed three weeks more to learn Morse Code and radio communications.

The Navy then sent me to an attack squadron in Virginia Beach, Virginia. The A6-A Intruder was a new plane at the time, and we had to learn to repair it and train to use the systems. Even though I was stationed close to Dick, he went to

Cuba before we could see each other, and I lost contact with him until many years later.

In September of 1966, after a few months of training, we were loaded aboard a C-130 and flown all the way across the country to San Diego, California, the home port for the carrier Kitty Hawk. I had never seen a ship before, let alone one as large as that one. Imagine 5000 men in an area ¼ of a mile long and only 8 stories tall eating, working, and flying jet aircraft from the flight deck which is about 110 feet above the water. It was love at first sight.

We went on a shakedown cruise up the West Coast of California, and we put ashore in Oakland. I was amazed at all the different types of people. It definitely was not Kansas any more. I am not sure I was confident I was on the same planet!

I was with a small group of guys going from bar to bar and in one I saw several girls arguing over whose turn it was to dance with a very familiar looking sailor. It was Joe Belski. No man in the world could start such a commotion with girls. I waited until he got out on the floor and I went and started to cut in. When he turned around and saw me, he grabbed me and hugged me! In California, especially the Oakland and San Francisco area, no one did more than glance at us.

"You do know they think we are gay!"

"No one cares, but I am really glad to see you!"

I left my group, and Belski and I sat and talked about where we had been and where we were going. He was on a light cruiser that was going to be part of our escort to Viet Nam. It was great to think we might be able to go on liberty together. Knowing the first port of call was to be Pearl Harbor, we agreed to meet at the closest bar to the Kitty Hawk as soon as we got off the ship. Also, we would leave a message with the bartender when we would be back if we missed one another. It worked like a charm.

The Kitty Hawk pulled into Pearl the day before my birthday, which is November 7th, in 1966. I was to turn 21 that next night at midnight and the bartender was going to let me order, but not drink, until midnight. There were so many friends from the ship that my table was full of free drinks.

The bar closed at 2:00 a.m. and between midnight and closing I do not remember how many, nor even <u>what</u>, I had to drink, but some-how I woke up in my clothes on board the ship in my own bunk with no idea how I got there. Thank the Lord for friends. I have never again been that wasted, and I do not even drink today. That night cured me!

Joe Belski and I found a little corner bar the next evening, after I was sober, a couple of blocks from the beach owned and operated by a young, gorgeous, raven-haired lady with blue eyes. It was startling to see such a beautiful woman in a bar, and I watched Belski "strike out" for the first and only time I ever knew.

She laughed with him and cut up with him, she even danced with him, but she never let him get fresh. Her bar seemed to cater to more of the base personnel instead of the sailors from the ships. It was quiet, and I liked it so much I would sit and visit while Belski would go down the beach and then come by and get me when it was time to go back to the ship.

The owner of the bar, Kathy Anderson, who was only a year older than me, had a nice, red and white 1957 Ford convertible hardtop. One night when Belski was busy she offered me a ride to the ship at closing. When we tried to start her car, I did not even hear it click.

I raised the hood, found the solenoid, and also a pair of pliers from the trunk. I had Kathy turn on the ignition and I jumped across the terminals with the pliers. She squealed and jumped behind me when I made sparks fly. However, it started right up when I got it to turn over and pumped the gas by hand on the carburetor. I got a breathtaking hug from Kathy for my effort. On the way to her house, we stopped at a large filling station which carried a few parts, and I purchased a new solenoid. After I fixed her car, we went to her nice little bungalow on the side of the hill overlooking the city.

"If you want to sleep on the couch, I will take you to the ship in the morning in time for your roll call."

"What will people think?" I asked with a smile.

"You will probably be famous, but only you and I will know the truth." We both laughed for I knew what she meant. Me getting out of her car in the morning at the ship was going to raise some eyebrows.

She took the day off the next morning, and I was free as soon as I reported in to my chief. I got out of her car and ran up the gang plank, saluted the flag, went to the shop still in uniform and reported to the chief I was sober and well. I tore off my clothes almost, grabbed a set of swim trunks, showered, put on a fresh uniform, and was at the quarterdeck within 20 minutes. I asked the OOD for permission to "go ashore", permission was granted, and as I started down the gang plank I saw there was a crowd around Kathy's car and she was sitting on the hood laughing with the guys. She knew most of them by name anyway from the bar. When she saw me she waved and the whole crowd of swabbies turned to see who the lucky guy was, or so they thought. The crowd parted to let me by and as I walked up to the car Kathy put her arms around me and kissed me. She held it just long enough for the cat calls to start. She was right. I was going to be famous!

Kathy and I spent the next couple of days together before my ship sailed. We went swimming and for long walks on the beach, she cooked for us, I tried surfing (almost drowned), bought a couple of flowered Hawaiian shirts, and when we kissed and I left her on the dock we promised to write.

She actually wrote first. I was surprised. I thought I was just a temporary friend. We began writing nearly every day. Mail call came several days at a time aboard ship, and it became a joke that my letters from Kathy were making his bag smell like her perfume!

Chapter Four

The first cruise I made in the fall of 1965 to the summer of 1966 the Kitty Hawk had A1-H Skyraider planes aboard. Those were prop driven aircraft, and were used for mostly troop support. However, on the 1966 to 1967 cruise, the Kitty Hawk was all jet aircraft. We had A4 Skyhawks for troop support as well as F4 Phantoms for defense and bombing missions. My squadron, VA 85, had the new A6-A Intruder which at the time was the world's only all weather bomber. It could launch from the deck of a carrier, fly in a monsoon by radar and a GPS system, bomb a preset target, and return to the ship.

The North Vietnamese had upped the ante somewhat by the time we returned to Viet Nam in November 1966, and in just over a month we lost most of our flyable planes to a new SAM, Surface to Air Missile, China had given them. So, just before Christmas the Navy pulled us off the front lines and sent us electronics techs and the planes to Japan to be updated with ECM, Electronic Counter Measures, to give a false echo for the radar launched missiles of the North Vietnamese. From that point we never lost another Intruder to SAMs. We lost a couple to ground fire later, however.

We were to be in Japan for at least 30 days for the refit. Kathy and I had been keeping in touch almost daily by mail, and she flew in and rented a small hotel room not far from Fuji Air Force Base while I was there.

Every morning on the base we could see Mount Fuji in the distance as we walked over to the chow hall. It was quite a sight because it rose up right out of the plain. It had plenty of snow from the Winter time of the year.

Kathy and I went shopping in the Ginza, or market district, in Yokohama and Tokyo. I purchased a Minolta 35 mm camera, and we went sight seeing on my days off. We had long talks about what our future would hold since I was due to get out of the Navy in June that year. I did not propose marriage, but things were pretty serious between us.

When it was time to go back to Yokohama to board the Kitty Hawk, Kathy saw me off at the train station. When she kissed me, all my friends clapped. No one had believed she was as pretty as I said, and everyone thought she was even better looking than I had said.

Our next port of call was Hong Kong. I loved the British being in charge for there were so many signs in English. I bought a Garrard turntable with an amplifier/receiver plus floor speakers and sent it all home. I was looking forward to playing records from my early Rock and Roll collection on it.

We were only there for 5 days, but I found Belski and we went to the China Fleet Club. It was run for the benefit of service personnel, and it was the best place to eat a steak. Afterward, we went bar hopping and wound up in a bar with mostly Chinese patrons. The band sang Country and Western songs by phonetics. Hank Williams never intended to have his songs sung in broken

English. Still, the musicians were good and we found a table and probably drank too much. At a table across the room was First Class Boatswain's Mate, Lester Burleson, the most hated person on the ship.

My run in with him was when I really had to go and I went into a restroom aboard ship and with the urinals all being used, I went into a stall with a commode. I raised the lid and did my thing, flushed it, and then a hand went around me and tried to grab my hat which was tucked into my belt. I pushed back and used my forearm to hit the thief in the face. I turned around and was ready to attack...it was Burleson.

"You are on report for using the commode instead of the urinal! Also, for striking a petty officer!"

"Sorry, old man. I heard you were sorta queer but I never thought you would steal a man's hat!"

"I wanted your hat so you would go with me while I made a report. It has your name and service number on it."

"First, I am not ship's company. You want to put me on report you have to go see my chief. I tell him what really happened and he is going to drop it anyway."

"You bloodied my nose. I will find a way to get even."

"So, guys, you heard that threat right?" I asked some of my squadron friends that had seen and heard it all. They all took a step closer and nodded affirmative.

"Get outta here, Burleson!" my six foot four Texas friend, Lanny, said.

"Look around. No one but airdales in here. You are about one step away from having your plow cleaned!"

Lester looked from angry face to angry face and decided a fist fight was not in his best interest. He looked at Lanny and me and said,

"We'll meet again!"

"I'll look forward to it!" smiled Lanny which made Burleson so red faced angry I thought he was going to have a fit. He was used to people cowing down. No one had ever stood up to the Boatswain's Mate aboard ship.

He did put Lanny and me on report, but we had 4 or 5 witnesses which told the same, true story, and my chief just filed it chapter 13. (The trash can.)

Now, back to the story.

A sailor sitting at the next table said out loud, "I would give a hundred American dollars if he did not make it back to the ship!"

A Chinese man in a black Ninja outfit came over in just a few minutes and whispered something in the guy's ear. I happened to see the guy reach into his shirt pocket and count out the money under the table and slip it to him. He thought no one saw him, but Belski and I did.

"What are we gonna do, Belski? He's a piece of work, but he is still an American sailor. We better follow him and make sure he makes it back to the ship."

Belski, who had some experience in this sort of thing on the streets of Chicago, said, "Let's wait out side. Someone sees us get up and go when Burleson does they will know we are watching."

Belski went out the door and started a conversation with a cab driver. Just a few minutes later, Burleson came out with a girl on each arm supporting him he was so drunk. Just before he got to the cab where Belski was, two guys dressed in black started coming down the sidewalk toward him. He never saw them until they were in his face. I saw real fear in his eyes and it almost sobered him up. Belski stepped between Burleson and the men and said loudly, "I got us a cab! Come on!"

One of the men reached for Burleson and Belski hit him on the side of the head with the palm of his fist hard enough to knock him down. The other man got into the Wushi, or Kung Fu, defensive position, and Belski told him, "I am a 32nd Degree Black Belt myself. I can hold you off long enough to get the cops here. We know what you are doing. Keep the money. Take your comrade and leave!"

He looked at us two determined sailors, picked up his buddy, and with a two-fingered salute to Belski he took off across the street and got into a black car and sped off.

I stood and held Burleson who had passed out from the alcohol and fear. I pulled two twenty dollar bills out of his shirt pocket and gave it to the girls. They had seen enough and would have left without pay. I had an offer of a "free one" for giving them the money. No idea what she meant, but Belski did and he just smiled. I knew I didn't want to know.

We tumbled Burleson into the back seat and I got in with him while Belski got up front. The cab driver took off driving like it was a race against a demon! He cut across lines of traffic with horns blaring and people yelling things in Chinese I did not want anyone to translate. I did understand the sign language from some of the drivers.

Amazingly, Belski was calm while I was freaking out!

"How can you be calm like that?" I yelled.

"I have my eyes closed!"

My short life passed before my eyes a couple of times before the cab skidded to a stop at the boat launch. They were just loading for the ride out to the ships, and we piled Burleson into the launch. No one wanted to sit too close to him and he had plenty of room.

The launch let off the Kitty Hawk personnel first. I hugged Belski and shook his hand. He had already told me he was shipping out for the States when we got back to the Philippines in a few days. A couple of ship's company sailors helped the still drunk Burleson aboard, and I waved to Belski one last time as the boat left the gang plank. I figured I would never see him again.

I had seen all I wanted to see of Hong Kong. So, for the next day I took pictures from the flight deck of brightly colored Chinese fishing boats and water taxis. I went up like most everyone and watched the preparations to leave port. I was standing on the front of the flight deck when someone called my name from behind me. It was Burleson.

"What do you want, Burleson?"

"Man, I just wanted to thank you for saving my life!" He stuck out his hand.

I looked at him solemnly for a few seconds to make sure he was sincere before I smiled and shook hands with him.

"You are still a piece of work, Burleson. I am not proud I even know you, but you <u>are</u> part of the family!" I smiled again and shook his hand one last time. As I turned to go he patted me on the back. I looked over my shoulder with a grin and said, "I am holding on to my hat this time!"

He laughed as I walked away.

"Tuck in that shirt, sailor!" I heard him playfully yell at me. I did not even look around. I just shot him the bird behind my back as I kept walking. I could hear him laughing all the way across the flight deck.

Chapter Five

Burleson was a changed man. He knew what would have happened to him if he had been kidnapped. For my part I did respect who he was and what he did aboard ship. Whenever we happened to meet in the passageway, a little smile and a nod was all that passed between us, but I had made a friend.

We started bombing around the clock when we got back on line in the China Sea. Joe Davis, the other flight deck troubleshooter, got hurt when a bomb rolled over his foot, and I had to run the flight deck by myself. I made sure all the electronic systems were up and ready for each plane before the flights took off, and I was the one which had to insert a"Remove Before Flight" flag in the bombardier navigator's seat as soon as they returned to the ship. The Intruder had an explosive charge which would destroy the aircraft if it was ever shot down and they removed the BN. The plane was full of radar and equipment that the Chinese and Russians would love to have had their hands on.

I slept 2 to 3 hours at a time usually draped over a bomb cart or sitting in a chair while the planes were out on a bombing run. I learned to drink Navy coffee so strong the spoon almost stood upright in it. However, after a week or so I was beginning to wear down. A corpsman friend gave me a handful of little white pills that were about the size of saccharin tablets. He told me, "Do not take more than 2 tablets every 12 hours!"

The pills helped me keep going, but there were times I was a zombie. We were finally told we only had 2 days of bombing left before we would stand down for repairs and replenishment. I took my last tablets and was wide awake for nearly 30 hours. When we were secured to go below I went and ate, showered, and fell into my bunk. I went to sleep about 4 in the morning according to my watch. I woke up and my watch said it was almost 4. I assumed it was 4 in the afternoon, but it was 4 in the morning! I had slept almost 24 hours! I never took those pills again.

Chapter Six

One of the most beautiful women in the world to me is a Swedish born lady actress by the name of Ann Margret. I had long been a fan when she came aboard the ship with Johnny Rivers to do a show. When she came aboard in the helicopter she had on a mini skirt. I put my 35 mm camera over everyone and took a once in a lifetime shot. However, when the pictures came back from the onboard darkroom, my negatives and prints were replaced with pictures of the engine room. I complained to my CO and we both tried to tell the smiling clowns at the processing center on the ship I had never been down in that part, I was an air dale. They said there must be some mistake. My CO said, "Yes, there is a mistake. I ever see the pictures in print or on your locker or whatever and you will be doing time in the brig. Is that still funny?"

They quit smiling, but we still never got the pictures. I shot some more of Ann Margret during the show, but I was so far away it was not the same.

Ann Margret was, and still is, gorgeous. All the veterans appreciated her attitude toward us. Not like the "want to be famous even if it costs people's lives" person that went to North Viet Nam.

We had a daily jam session of guitar players, a clarinet, a bass guitar and several singers on the hangar deck at night, and the guitar player which was traveling with the group came and sat in. After a few songs we were sitting and visiting with him about what it was like to travel with Ann Margret, and he told us about Johnny Rivers hitting on her constantly. It seems, however, she did not return the affection. I suppose when Elvis is your boyfriend it would be hard to take something less. I, for one, would have carried her bags in a heartbeat just to be near her.

We enjoyed the show and she was so gracious and personable. She won all our hearts. I was too far back to be able to get one of her dances or kisses, but if I could have it to do over, I would have stood there all day at the front until the concert started just to be up close and personal with my favorite movie star of all time.

Chapter Seven

Things could get crazy on board the ship when we were flying, but there was lots of free time when we were not. We worked shifts of 12 hours on and 12 hours off 7 days a week. If the planes were not flying I had lots of spare time. I learned to play a few songs on a guitar, played cards by the hour, and I bought a book to learn how to play chess.

I met Tom Irwin, an ordnance technician, from upstate New York. Chess became almost an obsession with us. We played game after game and he would patiently point out the nuances of the game until occasionally we could play to a draw. I even won a game once in a while, but Tom was a Junior Chess Master from the state of New York. He was way beyond average.

We pulled in to Subic Bay once and we went to the USO on base. There was a Japanese Chess Master playing about 20 games at a time. It did not take long of him walking around making quick moves to separate the men from the boys. Tom, Mr. Chess Master, and me were all that were left after a few minutes. I played to a stalemate, but Tom beat him! It was probably humbling to the Japanese man, but he shook our hands and bowed from the waist to both of us. I wish I had a picture.

In late May of 1967 the Kitty Hawk was making preparations to get underway for another tour of the South China Sea to drop more bombs on the jungle. I was asleep in my bunk about 5:30

a.m. when I felt and heard an insistent tapping on my bunk, and there was a flashlight shining in my face.

"Get that light out of my face!" I growled.

"Oops, sorry, son," I was instantly awake for it was the unmistakable, gravel voice of my squadron commander!

"Get your sea bag packed! You have to be in the Ready Room in 5 minutes. Put on your uniform. You are going home!"

I was out of my bunk and moving as if it were General Quarters and Battle Stations!

My sea bag was near and I had on my dress whites and was in the Ready Room standing at attention in 5 minutes flat!

"Sorry, sir, I didn't realize that was you," I started apologizing.

"I quite understand. That was rude of me," the Commander said.

"I know this is short notice, but I have orders from Senator Albert Gore to put you on the next plane back to the States," he continued. "I didn't know you knew Senator Gore."

"Actually, I don't sir. He has a son named Al Gore Junior that plays baseball with my younger brother. My dad and the Senator sit and visit in the stands while the guys are playing,"

"Well, if you ever meet him you tell him the only reason we were trying to keep you in the Navy is that we needed you. Put in a good word for me if you can. You do know our commissions are granted by Congress and we take notice when Congress speaks!" He was speaking to me as if he were really sweating Senator Gore coming back on him.

My head was spinning, everything was happening so fast, but I got on a bus in Subic Bay, Philippines, and traveled to Clark Air Force Base. We went to the air base terminal and got off, and I checked my sea bag to the Oakland, California, terminal which was the destination on my orders.

A couple of MP's escorting a Navy Lieutenant approached me and one of them said, "We need to talk to you."

I thought to myself, "Oh, Lord, they are going to send me back!"

"You and Lieutenant Bronson are the only Navy personnel on this flight. Would you put on hand cuffs and escort this briefcase and the Lieutenant back to the States?"

"I guess so," I answered trying to keep my voice from quavering.

"You and the Lieutenant will be the last on and the first off the plane. That should be a good thing."

"Okay," I said. "What if one of us has to go to the restroom?"

This big Marine MP smiled wickedly at us and said, "I guess you will have to just work it out!"

You gotta know that did not strike me near as funny as it did the two MP's. They handcuffed my right, and the Lieutenant's left, wrists together, patted me on the back and went off laughing uproariously. I suspect we were the topic that night in whatever bar they went to.

Lieutenant Bronson was a year younger than me and, after graduating from Stanford University in California with a degree in Physics and ROTC, he was inducted into the Navy and went to

Viet Nam as an attache to an officer on the Enterprise. Whatever was in the brief case he carried was Top Secret. I never figured it out whether it was all that important or they just did not trust him.

We neither one, thankfully, had to use the bathroom in the Philippines, but sure enough, at the International Airport in Japan we both had to go. Now, set this visual in your mind. Here I am, not left handed, and having to work very clumsily at going to the bathroom, finally get going and so does he. He seemed a nice enough young man, and we had a laugh when we agreed we were not going to help each other!

Everyone loaded and we were put on the very first row. I was seated next to a pretty, young Navy nurse. You ever tried to make time with a classy girl when you are in handcuffs? In my best, friendly, pickup voice I said, "Well, hello."

She glances at my handcuffs, sticks her nose up in the air and turns her back to me. She was probably thinking I was a very dangerous criminal to have to be handcuffed and escorted.

"Fine," I said to myself.

Luckily, it was okay to take off the cuffs while we were flying. Once out of the cuffs, the girl was amused at her mistake, and apologetic enough for the rest of the flight to be fun.

She was being transferred to Treasure Island and since that was where I was being processed, we met and went out a couple of times while I was in San Francisco. She had access to a car in which we dated, and the day I was to leave she drove a back way to the airport so I could beat all the other soldiers and sailors trying to fly home on standby just like me. I got a nice kiss, and I never saw or heard from her again.

I came home from Viet Nam in the first week of June in 1967 to Cookeville, Tennessee, close to where my parents lived at the time. My parents lived a few miles away in a small town named Carthage, Tennessee, which was the home of the afore mentioned Senator Albert Gore. After he got me out of the Navy to go back to school, I almost voted Democrat after that.

I had been at home for only a few days when my mother came and got me out of bed in the middle of the night to tell me there was a phone call for me from Hawaii. I only knew one person in Hawaii, and when I picked up the phone a familiar voice said, "Well, sailor, I haven't heard from you in a while. Now that you are out of the service, did you forget me?"

I was tongue-tied for a moment, but I was very glad to hear from Kathy.

"You know there is no one in the world who has ever seen you who could forget you! I still think of you."

"Okay, if I paid for you a ticket to San Diego could you come day after tomorrow for at least a few days? I am coming stateside on business, I have a nice hotel room, and I would love to see you."

"Let me ask my mother, but probably I can."

She laughed, but I was totally serious.

My folks took me to the airport in Nashville, and there was a round trip ticket waiting in my name. The trip to San Diego was a lot more fun than when I went to boot camp, trust me.

Kathy met me at the airport. She had her hair cut shorter and with her natural tan she was more beautiful than even I remembered. There were a lot of jealous guys in the airport terminal watching me kiss her, and then with her arm through mine, to walk out laughing and talking. It was apparent to everyone we knew one another well. Kathy had a large final settlement check from her ex-husband in the bank, and she was there in San Diego to close a deal for a larger bar in Honolulu.

She had leased for her stay in San Diego a new 1967 red, Hertz Mustang convertible. Although it was an automatic, it had air conditioning and a 390 cubic inch engine and could burn a hole in the wind for its time. I enjoyed the car <u>almost</u> as much as seeing Kathy.

From the airport Kathy let me drive and we went for a drive up above the beaches and as much as I liked Hawaii, I loved San Diego and it is a lot closer!

After the first few hours of catching up with what each of us had been doing, Kathy got a very solemn look on her face.

"Don, you know I love you. Would you be willing to come back with me and help me run the new bar? You have been in the Navy and we could have all the business we could handle."

It was a little overwhelming. Here was one of the most beautiful women around. She was rich and would make me rich, and we get to live in Hawaii. What could be better?

"What's the catch?" I asked quietly.

"I don't want to get married just now. We could still live together and share everything, but after a disastrous first marriage, I don't want the stress."

"I am not the same man you married the first time around. I love you and respect you. I would never do to you what he did."

"Is that going to be a problem? I think we have great times together. You are the only man ever to come into my bar which I cared about."

We were sitting across from one another at a small table on the patio by the pool. The wind caressed her hair just like I had done many times. Her blue eyes were filling with tears. She reached for my hand across the table, and we just held hands and looked at one another for a couple of minutes. The emotions for both of us were swirling around us warm and wet like the ocean.

"I don't know, Kathy. I have a life starting this summer in college at Tennessee Tech. It is something I have always wanted to do. I will be the first person in my family to go to college. Is it something we have to decide on our first night together?"

"Our time is being cut short, Don. I have a 6 p.m. flight tomorrow evening. I am so sorry to put all this on you."

"Can I have some time? It is not something I can take lightly. My entire future is at stake."

"We love each other. What else is there?"

"You know I can be spontaneous in lots of things, Kathy, but this is serious."

She was not used to not getting her way. No man probably ever said no to her before about anything.

There were two queen sized beds in the room, and I slept on one and she the other. I finally got to sleep early in the morning. I heard her get up, but I went back to sleep thinking she was only going to the bathroom. The click the door made when she left woke me.

On her bed was a note that said, "Dear Don, if you are having trouble making this decision, I will make it easy for you. I am catching an early flight back. The Mustang and room are paid for through this afternoon at 6. Enjoy. Love, Kathy." She walked out of my life without even a kiss goodbye.

On the bright side, I went ahead and got my things together and checked out of the hotel and the Mustang and me got to know each other well! I went from stop light to stop light a couple of times and was never beaten! I cruised all over the beach and the hills around San Diego. On the way home I think I was missing the car as much as Kathy!

Still, after I returned home, I called a few times, and even wrote a few letters, but she never answered any. It was over for her. If she had been willing to wait we could have been together holidays and summer vacations, but I suppose she was tired of waiting on men when she could have most by snapping her fingers.

Chapter Eight

My dad's job moved him that summer to Hot Springs, Arkansas. However, I was already enrolled at Tennessee Tech so I decided to stay for college. I bought a new 1967 GTO with part of my savings from service, entered college as a Junior with the credits from before on the GI Bill, found a part time job to keep gas in the car, pledged a fraternity, and proceeded to enter into the life style of the late 60's and the early 70's.

I installed an 8 track tape player with 4 speakers in the GTO. I bought flared jeans and slacks from J.C. Penney's in Nashville, Hush-puppy shoes, grew my hair down on my shoulders with a matching mustache, and thus entered mainstream youth society.

We all wanted to look different from our parents, but we <u>all</u> had long hair and a "uniform" of jeans and T shirts. We looked like one another, but we definitely did not look like our parents.

I wore my work clothes of slacks and an open collar shirt to school the first day of class to not have to go home before I went to work. I looked so much like the "establishment" the kids would not even sit next to me, but after I came the next day in a T-shirt and jeans, they accepted me.

At the small department store where I worked evenings and weekends, there was another college student that was in two of my classes, Tiffany Parker. She had long blonde hair (don't they always) she would toss to the side with a quick movement of her head. This allowed her to look with her peripheral vision at whatever inter-ested her so it didn't look like she was actually in-terested. I knew she watched me, but I played a game of my own and tried to never let her see me looking at her.

At the age of 22 with a new car, plenty of money, member of a fraternity, and a job, I had lots of friends. On Saturdays several of them, both guys and girls, usually would come by and visit me while they shopped at VanHorn's Department Store. In the days before the proliferation of Wal-Mart and the entrance of department stores into smaller markets, if one went shopping in a small town, it was to small, family owned, department and specialty stores for clothes and shoes such as VanHorn's Department Store.

The owner of VanHorn's, B. D. "Buddy" Davis, and Charles Hartman, the manager, one day asked me what I thought about the future of flare leg pants on campus. I told them they were very fashionable and popular, and the ones I bought I went all the way to Nashville, about 75 miles away, to purchase.

On my word that it was going to be hot, Buddy and Charles endured the laughter of their local friends in the clothing business and put in a good assortment of young men's, Farah brand pants and jeans in the new flared look. It was a runaway best seller. VanHorn's was inundated with students from the local college, Tennessee Tech, and all the local high schools. Fortunately, they had also backed up the initial order with one that could be shipped in a hurry. We went from a quiet little department store with moms shopping for school clothes to a boisterous, fervent youth happening every Saturday.

Buddy changed the wired in background music to the youth rock station, hired several students as part time sales people to help sell on Saturday, and we sold clothes. It was so busy on the men's side of the store that Buddy asked Tiffany to come over and help. She didn't mind at all, for it was "wall-to-wall" young people (mostly young men), and her looks and personality helped her sell. She was cool, self assured, and could fend off the most obvious sexist, chauvinistic remark, turning it into a nice sale without offending.

In just a few days we were good friends, but she was a sorority girl all the way. I never considered us a possibility, because she confessed her current boyfriend was rich and in the richest fraternity on campus. She thought he was going to ask to marry her, and she confessed to me she would marry him if he gave her a 2 carat diamond.

Buddy and Charles started wearing flared pants, open collared, silk print shirts under their sport coats, and worked a deal with a couple of the other stores to sell, at a minutely reduced price, flared pants and shirts to the same business owners that had laughed at the new "fad". I got a nice raise and a cash bonus once in a while. It was a heady time the several months before the other stores started carrying flared pants and nylon or silk shirts. The school year went by in a blur of classes, studying, work, and even a couple of dates. I just didn't have a lot in common with most college girls, and the year ended with me looking around.

One early summer Saturday, late in the afternoon, a short, little old man wearing a somewhat tattered dark suit, white shirt with a standup collar and string bow tie, came in and asked for a pair of black dress socks. I found an appropriate pair, told the man it would be twenty-five cents, and we proceeded to the checkout counter. I wrote up the sale in my carbon copy sales book, charged the requisite one cent sales tax, and asked the man for twenty-SIX cents. He very firmly reminded me that I had told him only twenty-five cents.

"No problem, Mr…" I hesitated.

"Mingus. Thurber Mingus," he replied.

"Well, Mr. Mingus, the price is twenty-five cents to you today," and I smiled. His eyes twinkled a little, but he only managed a smirk back. I realized he thought he had just bested me. He had. He counted out twenty-five cents from a coin purse filled with change, took his small bag, sniffed and walked out the door.

Buddy was laughing out loud as he came up to me. "I see you met Thurber Mingus," he said still laughing.

When I inquired about him, Buddy told me what little anyone really knew about him. He lived in a shack beside the railroad right of way on land owned by Mrs. Nellie Gentry. He stayed to himself in that shack and rarely ventured out except for shopping. Once in a while Mrs. Gentry, who happened to be my landlady also, would give him a ride to a big ridge overlooking the lake just a few miles outside of town. She told me later she usually provided a picnic lunch of fried chicken, homemade biscuits, tea and cake or pie. They would sit talking and watching the birds and the lake till late afternoon, and then she would take him home.

A little after six o'clock the Saturday I met Mr. Mingus, we closed the store as usual, and as I prepared to drive home I put the windows down on the GTO. It was a warm summer evening and I drove slowly along the streets of Cookeville toward my duplex apartment. I took, for me, an unusual drive along the railroad and happened to see Mr. Mingus walking slowly with a cane in one hand and his VanHorn's paper bag in the other. I slowed to keep pace with him.

"Hey, Mr. Mingus, can I give you a ride home?" I offered.

He turned and looked at me for a moment with no expression and said flatly, "MAY you?"

I blinked, rolled my eyes in chagrin at my obvious misuse of the English language, and looking directly into his eyes, said, "Okay, MAY I give you a ride home?"

With that same smirk as before, he said, "Yes, you may."

I reached and opened the door from my side. As he got in the bucket seat on the passenger's side, he looked around sniffing at the new car smell, and made an observation.

"I did not know they were putting the gear shift back in the floor now."

"Well, only on special models," I explained. I felt it was useless to tell him about the 400 cubic inch engine, the four speed transmission and almost 400 horsepower the GTO contained.

As if reading my thoughts, he said with another of his by now irritating smirks, "I happen to know what a hot rod is. I had a 27 T bucket with a hot flathead V-8 just before the war."

"WOW!" I exclaimed. "I love the old cars!"

"My dad," I explained, "is a mechanic. I left home after he would not let me buy a 1950 Ford Club Coupe that had already been nosed and decked. It had a '53 Mercury flathead with two Stromberg carburetors, milled aluminum Offenhauser heads, and Smitty mufflers. He was afraid I would have started running around racing and wind up wrapping it around a tree. Even now he wanted me to go to college first before I begin my life, but all I ever wanted as a kid was a neat car and a garage or a dealership of my own. My GTO I paid for myself out of Viet Nam savings, and I know he probably worries about me sometimes. What he doesn't know is just how much I appreciate my car, and this is one pampered Goat."

"Goat?" asked Mr. Mingus with raised eyebrows.

"Street slang for GTO. Affectionate term if you have one, and sour grapes if you don't," I laughed. For the first time the old man seemed to relax and he even smiled.

"Mr. Mingus, would you like to go out and eat with Mrs. Gentry and me tonight, my treat? I am taking her to Captain D's, that new fish place."

He REALLY smiled now. "I would be delighted, Mr…"

"Bond. James Bond," I said with a straight face and then quickly I smiled. "Just kidding. It is Wayne. Don Wayne." It got no response at all even though it really was my name. He probably never went to the movies.

My little landlady was happily surprised to see Mr. Mingus, and to find out he was going with us. They both got in the back of my two seater car for some reason. We went down the street with me driving the black GTO with my head up as if I were a chauffeur, and the little old giggling couple in the back were my charges.

At Captain D's Mr. Mingus turned out to be quite a charmer. He was well read and had been all over the world as a young man. He still did not offer much about himself, but he and Mrs. Gentry seemed to know one another very well and liked one another MORE than very well. It was a very enjoyable evening.

Afterward, when we got to Mr. Mingus's house, a true little one room shack, I hopped out of the car, opened the door, pushed the seat back forward, helped Mr. Mingus out and walked him to his door. As he started to go inside he opened his coin purse and held out a coin to give me a tip. As the door shut I looked in my palm, laughed out loud, and shook my head. It was a new, shiny penny.

The next day was Sunday. Mrs. Gentry asked would I go and pick up Mr. Mingus at 11:30 and bring him to our Sunday lunch. She warned me to not be late.

I was there exactly at 11:29. Mr. Mingus almost smiled at me as I pulled up. He was already standing at the entrance of the little walk up to his house.

"Been waiting long?" I asked a little tongue in cheek.

"Not real long, but thanks for being punctual," he replied with that smirk. This time it was accompanied with a twinkle in his eye, and I thought to myself we were making progress. He opened the door and seated himself with his walking cane between his legs. I put the car in gear and eased away from the curb.

"Mr. Mingus, what's your story?" I asked gently, as we drove slowly through town. "Neither one of us is from Tennessee, and from your accent I would guess up north and the Midwest, maybe Chicago. I had a great friend in the Navy from there and he had the same accent."

He looked straight ahead for a moment and smiled a small smile as if he were reliving some old memories.

"You are correct," he said, in that peculiar way he had of talking with no contractions. I knew there was a lot more to him than met the eye. "I am indeed from Chicago."

"My mother and dad were well to do until the crash of 1929. My dad lost everything and committed suicide in 1932. My mother crawled into the whiskey bottle and never came out. She died in 1934, and my grandfather on my father's side took me in. He was a rum runner for the mob and a pal of some not so nice people, like Siegel and Capone.

I became a numbers runner and a card shark by the age of 14. I became quite a bit of a ruffian also. My grandfather and his bodyguards taught me to fight, both in and out of the ring. Finally, after a brush or two with the police, he sent me to a military school in Pennsylvania for rich kids trying to keep me out of the life he was in.

He sent a bodyguard and a limo with me. I had to stay in the dorm of course, but the driver stayed in a nice hotel which I am sure was not hard duty. I went and stayed with him a lot at night and on my weekends. I kept myself in spending money by playing poker with him.

The first day of school the limousine driver, whose name was Louie, opened the door for me, and I got out in my expensive knee pants, blazer, sport cap and spats. Conversation stopped as the people looked at me. At first I thought I was being admired, but I suddenly realized they were looking at me as if I were from outer space!

One of the older boys came over and said, "Well, looka here! He musta just got off the boat." He had dirt hidden on his hand and wiped it on my blazer and then back handed my hat off my head.

Everyone was laughing as he reared back, pointed at me as he was looking at the crowd and they were laughing too. When he turned back toward me, I hit him in the nose with a good straight left jab and then followed it up with a roundhouse right cross that caught him right on the point of his chin just like my grandfather's bodyguards had shown me. He went down barely conscious with blood all over his face. I stood over him with both fists clenched yelling, "Come on, jack! You ain't nothing! I have seen and whipped REALLY mean guys in Chicago! <u>You</u> would be whipped by the <u>girls</u> in my neighborhood!"

I glared at all the other boys, "Anyone else want some of me?" They made a <u>big</u> walkway as I picked up one of my bags, and my huge limo driver and bodyguard had a scowling look of his own at the boys that made some of them turn and run. He picked up the remainder of my suitcases and carried them behind me up to my room."

"Good job, Thurber!" he laughed. "I guarantee you no one is going to mess with you after that!"

What I did not know was that the Dean of Men, Gus Langford, saw the whole thing. Mr. Langford was a retired boxer and was the coach of the football and the boxing team. Later he told me he had said to himself, "Finally, a leader!" Gus had to bite his tongue sometimes to not say anything inappropriate to all the spoiled little rich kids he had to almost bow down to every day. He told me he was so glad to find someone that would stand up to them.

Besides my grandfather, and Louie, the limo driver, Gus Langford was one of the few men I ever loved and respected. He came by my room, shook Louie's big hand with a big hand of his own, and explained to me that retaliation was only allowed in the boxing ring. However, he laughed at me whipping the biggest bully in the school. We were friends long into my adulthood.

I played football as the best, toughest, running back he had ever coached. I won awards for boxing both my Junior and Senior years. I was elected class president and "Most Likely To Succeed." I had several offers to play football from some big name Ivy League colleges, and I knew my grandfather would pick the best for me.

After high school I went to Yale for two years on his money and connections, but I hated the snobs and the bigotry and left school and came home. My grandfather, bless his heart, understood, and when I told him I wanted to see the world, he gave me some money and this old round top chest I keep by my side.

I went to England with a couple of well to do friends from college. We partied every night and slept or played golf or tennis during the day. When the war came, I went to South Africa with my friends and waited until it was all over.

By the time I came back to the States five years later, my grandfather was dead and no one knew I even existed. My aunts and uncles had fought over my grandfather's money until there was none left, and a couple even shot each other. It was sad to see them all end up that way after having so much earlier.

I roamed around a little on the money that my grandfather's secret trust was still sending me, and while spending some time at a hotel one summer on Lake Michigan I met David Gentry.

He was a rich tycoon from a place called Cookeville, Tennessee, and he was traveling with the most beautiful black haired, brown-eyed companion I had ever seen. That was not uncommon in those days. She had her own room of course, and she was there just to decorate his arm for activities. Yes, that girl was Nellie. I was smitten. She was his bookkeeper and claimed she was not "involved". We played tennis and I rowed her around on the lake, which was by the clubhouse, while her boss conducted his business. Mr. Gentry was in his early 50's, and Nellie was a sweet 25 year old.

Courting in those days was more frustration than gratification. It was several days before I even held her hand, and never in public. When told they were getting ready to go back to Tennessee, I put my arms around her, and not meeting with a lot of resistance, I finally kissed her!"

At that, Mr. Mingus looked out the windshield as if reliving that precious moment. I smiled a little to myself, and then pressed him as to what happened after the kiss.

"I told her I loved her and wanted to marry her," he continued. "She told me she loved me too, but confessed she was not free. David Gentry's wife had died a few months before and he had already asked to marry her after a little time. She was already engaged to him. She cried, kissed me, and walked away with my heart.

They left the next morning. She and David got married and I would not bother her. She had made her choice. No one, especially me, could fault her for taking the brass ring. I made and lost several fortunes in the next few years trying to forget her. Then, about ten years later, I heard her husband had passed.

I came to Tennessee in the early 50's just wanting to be alone I told myself, but I just wanted to be near Nellie. I wanted to leave Chicago because I was so dissipated and worn out. Without any means of visible support, I could not ask Nellie to marry me, and so, I moved into Nellie's little house and retired."

When I asked if he had any ongoing income, he said that he had a little, but he really had no wants and therefore did not need much money. I think he picked up on the fact I thought he was broke, and so he said, "You are a fine young man for what you do for Nellie and me. When the time comes you can have the keys to the chest."

I figured it was old clothes and maybe a few pictures. It would be interesting, but I forgot about it until years later when the will was read.

We had a great time at Nellie's lunch, and I drove him back to his little house and watched with a lot more respect as he walked up the walk. He turned and actually smiled and waved.

This page is blank to allow the

chapter to start on the right hand page.

Chapter Nine

Tiffany's boyfriend lived in Nashville, and after school let out for the summer he was at home working in his father's law office. She only got to see him on the weekends, and he had already missed the weekend before and it was only the second week of June. She told me once she missed going out every night.

One evening after work I happened to see her at the local Piggly Wiggly. I watched her picking out vegetables, and I was wishing she would squeeze me the way she did all the heads of lettuce. I wanted to talk to her, but I was game enough to make her notice me first. I went to the same aisle and I had my back to her trying to pick the best cantaloupe I could find. I could feel her behind me, and it was not too unlike being backed up to an open fireplace.

"Why, hi, Don," she said. "You do know the best way to pick a cantaloupe is to squeeze it and then SMELL it."

"Much the same way I pick up girls," I said with a straight face.

She smiled and looked at me for a moment before she burst out laughing.

I was enchanted watching the toss of her hair, the blue eyes sparkling, and a perfect set of white teeth framed with live coals for lips. She made my toe nails curl just looking at me.

"What am I going to do with you?" she said, still smiling.

I could think of lots of things, but I only offered one.

"Why don't you let me buy you a coke?" I said. She seemed to ponder the ramifications for a moment before she answered my prayers.

"Sure, why not? Follow me to my home and I will put up my groceries."

"Tell you what," I said. "I will stop and get rid of my cantaloupes at my apartment, and be there at your house by the time you get through putting up your groceries. I like the smell of them but it is sort of a drag in a new car."

"Great," she said. "See you there." She acted like it made her happy to finally be getting out of the house.

I went by my duplex, stashed the cantaloupes in the refrigerator, and sped off to Tiffany's house.

Tiffany's mother and dad were working people. Her mother worked at the local Wilson Sporting Goods factory, and her dad was a mailman. They were <u>very</u> pleased Tiffany's boyfriend was rich. They had raised their daughter well. She and I could be friends and even summer lovers, but if Tiffany's boyfriend, Bill, offered her a 2 carat diamond, she was his. There was no misunderstanding on my part.

Their house was a very clean, well-maintained tract house bought on the GI Bill when her dad came home from World War II. I pulled to the curb, got out and went up to the door. At my knock, her dad opened the door. He was very polite, and even cordial, I knew he liked the fact I was a veteran and drove a new car.

"Good evening, Mr. Parker," I said.

"Don," he said, and nodded his head with a smile. Tiffany seemed to hurry a little as she hugged him and almost pushed me out the door.

I opened her door to let her in, got in the driver's side and we left for the Shoney's Big Boy Restaurant. She knew why I was a little quiet.

"Don't mind my folks. They are a little wary of my male friends."

"Rightly so, I imagine, but they don't have to worry about me. Why I don't even like you," I laughed.

With one little phrase she saw through me to the core.

"Yes you do," she said quietly. Then she giggled, tossed her hair and asked to drive my GTO.

"Wait a minute," I protested. "I don't even let my mother drive my car."

"I am not your mother," she said sticking her tongue out at me. "Pull over and let me drive. I can drive a stick shift as well as you can."

To tell the truth, I probably <u>wouldn't</u> have let my mother drive, but Tiffany Parker, oh yeah.

I pulled over, we both got out switching seats, and as we passed by one another, she branded me for life with her hand as she patted me on the shoulder and said smiling, "Don't worry."

"Oh sure, that's easy for you to say. It is not your car."

However, she <u>could</u> drive about as well as me as she put the transmission in first, let out the clutch, and took off, chirping the tires just a little as she shifted from first gear to second. She drove smoothly, shifting easy as if she too appreciated the GTO.

We didn't pull in at Shoney's. I didn't say a word. I just shook my head to myself and let her go. We headed south out of town on the open road toward Sparta, a little town about 15 miles away. Even on the few curves we encountered in the road, she could handle the car very well, and I began to relax. With The Credence Clearwater Revival playing on the 8 track through the 4 speakers, all the windows down on the hardtop, Tiffany's hair in the breeze, there was nothing wrong with the world for that moment.

She drove to the Dairy Queen in Sparta where we ordered milkshakes and foot long hot dogs. I held them while Tiffany drove a few miles to a place called "Lookout Point" which overlooked the town. Lots of couples went up there to see the city lights and to make out. All the mothers told their daughters, "If a guy takes you there, look out!"

It was way too early for lovers, and we had the place to ourselves as we sat in the car listening to the music and watched the sun set, not saying very much while we ate.

I pulled out the tape and turned the radio on and dialed it to the new FM station playing stereo music from the college campus. A lot of the songs were a little fast, but Blood, Sweat, and Tears finally came on and sang the words,

"I lost at love before. Got mad and closed the door."

I stared out the windshield for a moment, and when I turned to look at Tiffany she was staring at me in the semi-darkness.

"Who was she?" she asked quietly.

"You women," I smiled. "You assume everything is about you."

"Well?" She wouldn't let it go.

"Okay," I said. Tiffany settled back into the seat with a self satisfied smile because she was making me open up.

"She owned a bar in Hawaii. As we went to Viet Nam usually in November, we pulled into Pearl for about a week to replenish each time we went over. I was there twice, but I didn't meet her until the second trip just before I got out. I found her bar to be quiet compared to the ones on the beach. She was two or three blocks from the beach, and catered to service personnel from the base more than the fleet sailors. I became a regular and she and I would sit and drink at the bar while she waited on customers. Believe it or not she seemed to want to talk as much as I did."

"I don't believe it," Tiffany said.

"Do you want to hear about this or not," I growled, teasing her. She sighed, put her head back on the seat and closed her eyes smiling.

"She was the divorced wife of a Naval officer that gave her the bar and went back to the States without her with some bimbo," I continued. "She was a beautiful half Hawaiian and half American with jet black hair and light blue eyes that could turn gray if you made her mad." Tiffany rolled her eyes.

"The ship was headed to Viet Nam in about three days, and we were closing down the bar as usual. She was going to give me a ride to the ship, but when we went out to her car it wouldn't start. She drove a very clean 1957 Ford Fairlane convertible hardtop. I opened the hood and told her to try to start it. It did not make even a small click.

Remember, my dad is a mechanic. Ford cars of those early years have a separate starter solenoid up on the side of the engine compartment. I took a pair of pliers she had in the car and told her to turn the key on. She watched as I jumped across the solenoid. She squealed and hid behind me when I made a spark, but she jumped up and down and hugged me when it started. I got a big kiss that lasted a little longer than either one of us intended, and it left us both a little breathless. You won't like this part," I laughed.

"Why not? I am sure it is mostly made up anyway," she countered.

"Actually, no it isn't," I said. "We went to her house after I bought a new solenoid and fixed her car. I spent the night on her couch."

She tilted her head to one side, looked at me, and said wryly, "Oh yeah? I knew it was made up." She shook her head.

Pretending not to notice, I went on. "She had me at the ship a little before 8 a.m. for me to make roll call. She waited while I went in, made muster, showered, changed, gathered up a few clothes including a swim suit and went to meet her. Although it might have only taken 20 minutes, there was already a small crowd of sailors around her car with her sitting on the hood smiling and chatting. No need to be jealous, for when I came down the gang plank and she waved at me, the crowd parted like the Biblical Red Sea did for Moses to see who I was. As I walked to meet her, there was a lot of murmuring and cat calls going on from the guys for they all knew both of us. She gave me a big kiss on the mouth and held it just long enough to make me a hero for the whole ship."

"Ugh!" cried Tiffany. "Too much information. I can guess what happened for the last couple of days you were in port. What happened after you sailed?"

"We wrote back and forth nearly every day, and she flew to Japan for a few days while I was temporary duty there in January outfitting the planes for some new gear. After my tour ended in June, she met me in San Diego for what was supposed to be a week."

"But that was just last summer!" she exclaimed. "What happened?"

"Her folks are in Hawaii, she already has a lucrative business there, and I was already enrolled at Tech. I didn't want to live in Hawaii, and she got mad and went home because I wouldn't fly back with her. She gave me an ultimatum. As a man, there are a lot of places a pretty face and soft hands can <u>lead</u> me, but I am not going to be <u>pushed</u> without a fight. I have not heard from her. Pretty stupid, huh?"

"Did you try to call her?" Tiffany asked.

"Of course, but she would not talk to me. I tried writing for a few months, but she hasn't answered if she even read them. I am sure she has moved on," I said sadly.

Truly moved, Tiffany put her arms around my neck to console me and suddenly we were kissing passionately. We broke the kiss with both of us trying to catch our breath, but she was still in my arms as she laid her head on my chest.

"I am sorry, Tiffany. I have wanted to kiss you for a long time."

I held her tight for a moment and then let her go. I opened the door and said, "I will drive you home."

It was quiet in the car as we drove back through Sparta and towards Cookeville. I drove with my hand on the floor shift knob. Somewhere about halfway back, she put her hand on mine and left it until I had to downshift when we got to her street. At her door she hugged me quickly and went inside. I drove off looking back in my rear view mirror telling myself she would never let me see her again.

Chapter Ten

I saw Tiffany on Saturday at work, but she only smiled at me. She made no move to talk. So, I didn't push it. There were so many unresolved feelings on my part I did not know what to do but wait.

Fortunately it was a busy day. I never even had a chance to be near her. Tiffany's boyfriend, Bill Price, came in just before closing time to tell her he would be waiting in the car. She glanced at me as she nodded okay to him. Cool me, I told her to go on and I would lock up. I locked the door behind them, put up the money, checked all the doors, the thermostat, and shut off the lights.

I went home and fixed myself a Coke with ice from my refrigerator's freezer compartment. I pulled the lever on the ice tray and spilled nearly every one of the cubes all over the counter. I filled my glass from the cubes on the counter, refilled the tray and put it back. I pulled out a record by Ray Charles, put it on the Garrard turntable I had sent home from Japan, and lay down on the couch to listen. When "Born To Lose" came on I knew I had to do something, but I didn't know what. I didn't want to go out. I could not take a chance on seeing Bill and Tiffany together. Mrs. Gentry and Mr. Mingus were out eating together, and I hadn't been invited. On top of that, it started to rain hard. It was a perfect night to have the blues.

About 9:30 Ray Charles had given way to Boots Randolph and his sax. Just as "Harlem Nocturne" came on there was a knock at the door.

It was still pouring a steady downpour as I went to the door wondering to myself who could be crazy enough to be out visiting on a night like this.

I opened the wooden door and there stood Tiffany crying. Her hair was flat and wet, she was soaked and shivering. Her mascara was running. She was beautiful.

When I opened the screen door to let her in, she was barely inside when the dam burst and she hugged me with all her strength as she started sobbing. I looked around for Bill, but I saw that she had driven over in her own car. I just held her as I closed the wooden door with my foot, and let her cry.

After a few minutes she had calmed down enough for me to lead her to the couch and sit down with her. My arm was still around her with her head on my shoulder as she took ragged, crying breaths.

"Bill had to go back to Nashville tonight..." she sobbed. "I couldn't wait for him to leave..." another sniffling sob. "Oh, Don, what am I going to do?" One last sniffling sob, and then she drew in and blew out a deep breath.

I suppose I hoped I knew what was coming next, but I wanted to hear her say it.

She looked up at me with her wet hair framing her face, mascara streaming, tears and rain in her face and whispered, "I love you."

She pushed me back on the couch and started kissing me hungrily all over my face. I pushed her back and sat us both up.

"Whoa, whoa, whoa!" I almost shouted. "Slow down. You can't do this to me. I am not one of your college boyfriends."

"Please," she whispered again.

"No! Know that I love you too, and I am not rejecting you at all. In fact I am crazy for you, but let's wait."

I made her tell me the whole story. She and Bill went out to eat, and afterward went parking, but she didn't kiss him the way she used to. He knew something was up, and she broke down and told him she had met someone and was going to see other people. He said that was fine with him and that actually he had been dating one of Tiffany's girlfriends that lived in Nashville. At that, she got to cry and be the "victim" and Bill left in a hurry. All of a sudden she started to laugh out loud at the irony of it all.

"Okay, so why are you crying?" I asked.

She started sobbing again. "Because I didn't get to look nice for you when I told you I loved you," she cried.

It was my turn to laugh. "You have got to be kidding me," I said. "You look beautiful to me just the way you are."

Later, I held my umbrella for her while I got soaked in the pouring rain. I let her take the umbrella so she wouldn't get wet again when she got home. I stood there until the tail lights on her car disappeared in the rain. I stood with both hands raised, barefoot in my jeans and t-shirt, my hair matted from the rain and yelled, "What a beautiful night!"

Chapter Eleven

Tiffany and I agreed to keep a low profile about our relationship. So much so, that we would meet at different places after work or during the day to be together. Her parents were hopeful that Bill and Tiffany would get back together, and if they saw too much of me, I imagined they would try to keep us apart.

I came back to my apartment one afternoon a couple weeks later, and there was a note from Mrs. Gentry for me to come and see her. I knocked on her door and she told me she was glad to see me and asked if I would help her move Mr. Mingus to the other side of my duplex. She had had an offer to sell the property containing his house and she thought she might. I moved the few personal belongings Mr. Mingus had into the other side of the duplex, which included a few clothes, a suitcase, and a very heavy round top trunk that was locked. Mrs. Gentry even made his bed while he watched and then bragged on the great job. He winked at me behind her back and we both smiled.

Afterward, Mrs. Gentry told me, as we sat on the front porch sipping iced sun tea, Wendell Dixon had been the one that called and wanted to know if she would sell her property along the railway. She thought he was very pushy and told him she would have to think about it. He wanted her answer soon he said.

Wendell Dixon was an aggressive, real estate developer in Cookeville at the time, and owned much of the cheap private, and some of the commercial, property in town. Mrs. Gentry claimed her husband and Dixon were enemies. Her husband believed he was a crook and did not trust him. He would find rental property, buy it and raise the rent as much as he could on the hapless tenants to gain a profit. Having the school nearby gave him a ready, over priced market to the college kids. Dark rumors surrounded the man's dealings, and he was the only man in town with bodyguards. He had offered Mrs. Gentry $30,000.00 for a 40 acre plot on the edge of town alongside the railroad on one side and the Interstate on the other. Since it was not really suited for houses, Mrs. Gentry was thinking she might just get rid of it. She also liked the idea of having Mr. Mingus close by. I told her not to do anything and I made her promise until I checked all this out.

I went to work a few minutes early the next day to talk to Buddy, my boss. I asked him why Dixon would want that particular property, especially since it displaced Mr. Mingus. The town was a few years away from expanding onto that property and incorporating it. It interested Buddy too, and he promised to be discreet about asking around about it.

I went on to work as usual, and just as we were locking up Buddy asked me to come to his office. He turned the blinds so no one could see in even though we were upstairs with the door locked. He was very excited about what he had found out.

Buddy's brother, Richard Davis, was the Prosecuting Attorney for the county and handled the city of Cookeville's legal interests. He had told Buddy that Wal-Mart was interested in that particular property because of the ease of entrance along the interstate. That was interesting, but the rumor was from one of Richard's friends that Dixon had gone to Wal-Mart and said he owned the property already and the price to Wal-Mart was for 800,000.00. He was really pushing Mrs. Gentry to sell to consummate the deal. He stood to make a very substantial profit in 1970 dollars.

As soon as I got home I went to see Mrs. Gentry and advised her not to sell to Dixon. She could sell to Wal-Mart herself through her lawyer and she would have enough money for her and Mr. Mingus to take a cruise if she wanted. That seemed to please her as she smiled and then blushed at the thought.

Mrs. Nellie Gentry was the "trophy bride" of David Gentry, a very wealthy local land owner. His lineage could be traced back to the founding fathers of Cookeville. Nellie had worked in his office as a receptionist and bookkeeper. He had been a widower for over ten months when he proposed to her, and the romance was a soul mate match for both of them. When he died he had had no children and left it all to Mrs. Gentry, who had been the light of his life. She really had no idea what all she did own in property and stocks and depended on Richard Davis, who was the only lawyer her husband trusted, to take care of her estate.

The next day I went to see Richard Davis at his office. Even though I did not have an appointment, I was ushered right in for he knew of me through his brother, Buddy. After the usual greetings and pleasantries which included me refusing a cigar, we sat down with me on one side of the largest wooden desk I had ever seen and him on the other.

Mr. Richard Davis had a very direct way of looking a person straight in the eyes when he was talking that made one want to tell the "truth, the whole truth, and nothing but the truth, so help me God." Just him looking directly at me with his dark brown eyes pinning me in my chair, made me want to confess all my past sins including my somewhat clandestine relationship with Tiffany. Somehow I managed to keep my composure, and after telling myself I had nothing to worry about, he smiled. Oddly, he had a very boyish, charming smile, and I liked him immediately. Richard lit up a huge, imported cigar and listened silently to what I had found out about the deal for Mrs. Gentry's property and I questioned how best to guard her from Dixon. He said he was impressed that I never even asked about a way for me to profit, but I was only interested in protecting Mrs.

Gentry. He blew a smoke ring while I talked. He had his head tilted back and I was hoping he was listening.

"What are you taking out there at Tech, boy?" he asked in his bourbon smooth Southern drawl.

"I am majoring in Business Management and pre-law, sir," I returned his steady gaze trying hard not to sweat, cry, run away or a hundred other cowardly options. Somehow I found the courage to just sit there and visit man to man, a benefit of having been in the military.

"You gonna run your own business someday?"

"Yes sir, but I actually want to practice law someday like you," I said.

The smile was gone for a moment while he studied me with those eyes to see if I were trying to "suck up," and apparently he was satisfied with what he read in me for he smiled that boyish smile again and said, "I concur with my brother Buddy. You are all right. You'd do to take along."

Richard explained to me only he had the Power of Attorney on Mrs. Gentry's properties and he had already been approached by Wal-Mart and Sam Walton himself. His deal with Wal-Mart included not only the property in question, but some add-ons of enough land for a huge warehouse and for a right of way that made the deal a cool 2 million dollars to Mrs. Gentry for the land. He was going to make her the richest lady in town while also cutting the unscrupulous Dixon out of even a penny. He had already drawn up the necessary papers and all he needed was Mrs. Gentry's signature, and he was going to hand her a check. He even called Mrs. Gentry while I was there and made an appointment for her to be in his office at 10 o'clock the next morning. In a really nice gesture toward me, he had told Mrs. Gentry to be sure and bring me to the proceedings.

He walked me to the door and in parting he asked, "How much college you got left, boy?"

"I will be a Senior in the Fall, sir," I responded.

"Let me think on some things. I might be willing to help you," he said and patted me on the back as he opened the door. There was that smile again.

At the door I extended my hand to shake hands. He had a very firm grip and like most genteel Southerners he appreciated a man's firm handshake in return. In the days when a man's handshake was his bond, a firm hand shake could go a long way.

I hurried back to Mrs. Gentry's and she was excited that Mr. Richard Davis wanted to see us. Even under her prodding I refused to tell her what was going on. I did not want to even run the risk of displeasing Mr. Davis. I told Tiffany that night Mrs. Gentry and I had the appointment and I promised to tell her all the sordid details as soon as it was over. Again, however, the most she got out of me was that I said it was some ordinary business and I was going to drive Mrs. Gentry to Mr. Davis' office.

The next morning I dressed in a sport coat and tie and was ready by 9:30. I drove the GTO around to the front of Mrs. Gentry's house and she and Mr. Mingus were sitting on the porch. She had her purse clasped in her lap with both hands. She stood up and smiled when she saw me, and politely said thank you as I opened the door for her. We waved to Mr. Mingus as we left, and neither of us spoke much as we drove to City Hall and Mr. Davis' office.

We were greeted by Mr. Davis' secretary, Jennifer, and as soon as she announced us to Mr. Davis, she ushered us into his office. Mr. Davis was sitting with two men at a table and all rose as Mrs. Gentry was introduced by Mr. Davis.

"Nellie Gentry, this is Mr. Sam Walton of Wal-Mart, and his son."

I was very impressed at how down to earth Mr. Walton was, and how polite he treated Mrs. Gentry. We all sat down at the table with me the farthest from the end where Mr. Davis sat. He smiled to see me in a tie and coat.

"Nellie, Mr. Walton and I have hammered out a deal for your property along the railroad and at the edge of town. It is a little more beneficial to you than your other offer, and I think you should take it," he said and he smiled.

"Thank you, Richard," began Mrs. Gentry. "I trust you to make the best deal possible you know that. I sorta figured this is what the appointment was about, but Don would not tell me any particulars."

Mr. Davis turned and smiled at me and nodded his head approvingly as if to say, "Well done." I knew I had done the right thing in not telling Mrs. Gentry the truth she was going to be rich.

"Mrs. Gentry, you don't know the offer on the table today?" blurted Mr. Walton.

"No sir, but I trust Mr. Davis made a deal that looked out for my best interests. He would make the best deal he could I am sure," she said and smiled warmly at Mr. Davis.

"I think you could say that," and Mr. Walton also smiled at Mr. Davis

"Mrs. Gentry can I get you a glass of water or anything before we get down to business?" asked Mr. Davis.

"Thank you, but no, Mr. Davis," she responded. "I hate to take up much of your time. However, I would like to know the final figure you came up with."

"Mr. Davis, may I handle this part?" asked Mr. Walton. He opened a black leather portfolio, pulled out a check, and put it on the table in front of Mrs. Gentry on the opposite side from him.

Mrs. Gentry smiled at him and picked up the check. Her eyes flew open wide, her mouth made a perfect letter O, and she dropped the check back on the table. She looked at it, blinked, and picked it up again in a trembling hand.

She looked first at a grinning Mr. Davis, then back to a grinning Mr. Walton and his son, and then to a grinning me.

She asked Mr. Walton in a trembling, small voice, "Is this check for real?"

"Oh, yes mam," said Mr. Walton. "I came all the way from Arkansas to make you a millionaire!"

"Richard," croaked Mrs. Gentry.

"Yes, mam?" said Mr. Davis.

"May I have that glass of water now?"

After Mrs. Gentry signed the papers, we all stood and clapped. Mrs. Gentry cried, and I had tears on my face too. If anyone deserved a break like this it was Mrs. Gentry.

Mr. Davis, Mr. Walton, his son and me, all escorted Mrs. Gentry across the street to The Citizen's Bank to deposit her check. Mr. Anderson, the bank president, almost fainted when he saw the check. He even got up and offered Mrs. Gentry HIS chair while she filled out the deposit slip. There were lots of smiles and tears in the bank that day.

Chapter Twelve

The next two weeks or so were crazy. Mrs. Gentry asked Mr. Mingus to marry her, and she, Mr. Mingus, Tiffany and I went to the court house together the day they got married. Tiffany and I signed the marriage license as witnesses. Afterward, we all went to the Palace hotel in downtown Cookeville, and celebrated with champagne. It was the first time I had seen Mrs. Gentry take a drink, but she held it pretty well. There were lots of blushes every time I saw her and Mr. Mingus look at one another. Several well-wishers came by and paid their respects to the happy couple. About midnight, Mrs. Gentry and

Mr. Mingus said goodnight and went upstairs for their wedding night.

Noticing a faraway stare at the departing couple from Tiffany, I stated, "Makes me almost want to run out and buy a 2 carat ring."

"You know, the truth is, you might could have me with a cheaper ring."

"Let me get this straight. You would marry someone for less? I don't want some cheap thing for MY wife!" I joked.

She kicked me under the table and said, "Fine. Don't come around and ask for <u>my</u> hand without at <u>least</u> a 2 carat diamond!"

I looked at the ceiling for a moment with my tongue in my cheek making a small mound on my jaw as if I were contemplating something serious, and said, "At what age would you consider yourself an old maid?"

"Just don't wait too long, smart alec. I don't want to be having to train somebody else."

"Oh," I smiled. "You mean how to fetch, grovel, and bow."

Giggling out loud she said, "See, you are getting smarter already."

Outside her house, I turned off the engine and left the radio volume low.

"They looked happy, didn't they?" Tiffany murmured with her head on my shoulder.

"I think it is great for them to find one another at their age. True love is hard to find at any age."

She gazed into my eyes for a moment and then quickly kissed me. She would not wait for me to open her door. She jumped out and ran up the steps onto the front porch. She turned at the door, waved, blew me a kiss with a smile, but I thought

I saw tears on her cheek before she went inside. I stared at the closed door for a moment, and wondered to myself, "<u>Now</u> what?"

Chapter Thirteen

The happy couple, Mrs. Gentry and Mr. Mingus, left on a month long cruise the next day after the wedding. I was given the keys to everything except Mr. Mingus's trunk. The day after they left, as usual I was up early having my coffee when the phone rang. It was Jennifer, Mr. Davis' secretary.

"Mr. Wayne, can you come into the office this morning about 10:00 a.m.? Mr. Davis would like to talk to you."

"Sure," I replied.

I was at the office, no tie, but I had on a sport coat over a dress shirt and slacks. I was there a minute or so before 10, and Jennifer was on the phone. I waited, but she put her call on hold and told me to go on in Mr. Davis was expecting me. I was impressed. I had her permission, but I knocked anyway.

"Come in, Mr. Wayne," boomed Mr. Davis. I opened the door and he had already stood and come around his desk. He shook hands warmly and motioned for me to come to the big table and have a seat. He laid the folder aside he was carrying and smiled at me. "Last couple of weeks was really crazy, wasn't it? I didn't get a chance to visit much with you."

"How's the Tech football team gonna do this year?" he asked, making small talk before getting down to business.

"Hopefully well," I countered. "Last year's 7 and 3 record may be bettered this year."

"You know," he said quietly, as we both watched a perfect smoke ring rise towards the ceiling. "Every fall we listen for the cannons. You can hear them all over town and miles around. Tech shoots off those two cannons when they score, and if there are lots of them going off we know they are doing well. If not, we know what is going on there too." He stopped and looked at me almost like he had forgotten why I was there.

"Something has happened in your behalf that you may really like," he began. "Mrs. Gentry wants for me to give you a little something for not letting her sell the Wal-Mart property to Dixon as a token of her appreciation. You know her well enough that you can appreciate the fact she felt a little embarrassed doing this herself. So, she asked me to do it while she is out of town."

He fastened those eyes on me and opened the folder and handed me an envelope. I recognized Mrs. Gentry's perfect calligraphy on the outside where she had written my name.

"You know, Mr. Davis, there was never anything about me in my doing what I did. I am making ends meet with enough to take Tiffany out. I am content."

In a very gentle voice he leaned toward me and said, "I know, boy. That is why this is a most joyful occasion for me and Nellie. We believe you have a good heart. I will be glad to see you get into law school. We need good men to replace us old codgers." He smiled and looked like a school boy in on a good joke. "Now, open the cotton-pickin' envelope!"

I ripped open the envelope and in it was a check made out to me in the amount of

$750,000.00. It was my turn to blink. "Is she sure this is what she wants to do? Can she afford this?" I said.

"Trust me, my boy. She has many times that amount and she wants you to stay in Cookeville. You do know she knows about you and Tiffany, don't you?"

"I am sure by now it is not much of a secret to anyone," I smiled.

"This ought to give you a little head start on your plans in life, Don. You can finish college and do whatever you want to do."

"That is a lot of money to me, Mr. Davis. I don't know what to say. I certainly never even thought something like this would happen to me. Would you escort me to the bank? It must make Mr. Anderson's day every time he sees us coming!" We both laughed at the remark, and he went with me while I set up a very nice savings account with most of it. I put 10,000 of it into my checking account. Mr. Davis smiled at me and winked. He knew I had to go jewelry shopping.

I drove the GTO back to Tiffany's house, and asked her if she wanted to go eat. She greeted me with a kiss and rode with her head on my shoulder to downtown.

"It is a little early. Just for grins, do you want to window shop at Metcalf's Jewelry Store?" She lifted her head up and looked at me with a look of wonder of why I could possibly want to go there with her. We had looked a couple of times, but she knew I was quickly bored because I could not afford the ring she wanted. "I thought I might get us matching silver bracelets or something." I smiled.

"Fine," she smiled back and stuck out her tongue at me. "Whatever."

What I didn't know was that Mr. Davis had already tipped off Mr. Bullock, the manager. He was always smiling, but this time he was grinning "ear to ear!"

Tiffany pulled me straight to the engagement rings. She had Mr. Bullock pull out a tray of the biggest diamonds I ever saw. Tiffany picked up a 2 carat solitaire ring, while I toyed with one that had a 3 carat center diamond and a ring of small ones around the outside that made it look huge.

Diamonds that size seem to have an internal glow all their own. I held it up and marveled at the multi-color lights from the prism effect on the wall, the counter, and my shirt. I thought to myself that no wonder Tiffany wanted one. Tiffany put on the 2 carat ring and held out her hand.

"What do you think?" she asked in mock "let's get this one" tone.

"You know, Tiffany, the size of the ring is not what marriage is all about. If I asked you to marry me, and I didn't want to give you a 2 carat ring would you still marry me?" I asked.

"Are you asking me to marry you?" she asked coyly.

"Tell you what, put on this 3 carat diamond ring, and let's see what it looks like." I took the ring, slid it on her ring finger, and got down on one knee. The ring was flashing in the light, Tiffany was suddenly very quiet, and I figured she was thinking I was kidding and for the moment she was not amused.

I had tears in my eyes as I held her hand tight. "Tiffany Parker, will you accept this ring and marry me?" I whispered.

"I would marry you regardless of the size of the ring, Don," she cried. She pulled me up to my feet, kissed me hard, and then, realizing everyone was staring and smiling at us, she pushed me away a little, blushing a deep red. She stared for a moment at the ring and then started to take it off.

"Wait. Is this ring not okay?" I asked.

She looked at me as if to tell me I was losing my mind. I grabbed her hand and said, "This is the ring I want you to have. I want you to know that I love you more than your old boyfriend."

"Oh, Don. You men don't know the value of things like this. This ring costs more than your GTO. You are still in school and working part time. How in the world do you think you can afford that ring?" she asked with a little crushed smirk.

"Hey, they will take a check," I said to Tiffany, who rolled her eyes as if I still did not understand what she was trying to tell me.

Looking at Mr. Bullock, who was smiling as if he were getting ready to burst, I said, "Mr. Bullock, you would take a check from me for this ring, wouldn't you?"

"Oh, yes," he purred, for he knew I had plenty of money even if he did not know how much. "And might I add, only a beautiful girl like Tiffany could wear a ring like this and her ring pale into comparison with her gorgeous beauty."

"Well said, Mr. Bullock," I laughed. "You took the words right out of my mouth." I lied for I don't talk like that. He just smiled.

Tiffany was freaking out. She looked at me, and was questioning me with her furrowed brow.

"But," she hesitated. "How?" She had such an expression of wonder on her face as if she were being asked to believe in Santa Claus.

"You will have to trust me, baby, but if you will marry me, the ring is yours!" I put my arms around her, but she began jumping up and down and squealing.

"Yes, yes, yes!" as she squeezed me in a bear hug and kissed me so hard that it was MY time to blush.

Everyone in the store, including the patrons, were clapping their hands, whistling, and carrying on with the women crowding around and wanting to see the ring. Mr. Bullock wrung my hand in appreciation as I handed him a check for the ring. It was expensive, even with a deep discount for Mr. Davis. It was a glorious moment.

In the car a few minutes later, all Tiffany could do was sit with her hand in her lap and stare at the ring. Finally, she asked, "Don, what have you done? Are we going to be in trouble?"

In a very straight face I said, "I gave the girl I love an engagement ring."

"Let's take it back," she said earnestly.

"We can't. I am sure Mr. Bullock has already cashed my check."

I looked straight ahead for a moment, and then pulled the car over to the curb. I put my right arm around her shoulder, took her ring hand with my left, and said, "I don't know what your family is going to say, but I do love you and I want to marry you."

She giggled, "Mother will just die. She told me, when she saw how happy I was, that the ONLY reason to marry is for love. She was concerned we would have to live from pay day to pay day like she and Daddy. However, she said she had two men too which had wanted to marry her early on. She went on and said she had turned down the money also, and had married for love. She had smiled at my expression, but told me she loved Daddy and that she would do it again. She even confessed to me you would be welcome in the family. MY question is, how can you afford it?"

"Some money came in unexpectedly, and I wanted to surprise you before I told you about it. We can get married whenever you wish, and we will be able to live very well, trust me."

She snuggled up against me and said, "Good answer!"

As we drove up to Tiffany's house we both noticed Bill Price's new Jaguar. It was a British Racing Green convertible, and he had bragged to Tiffany he was outfitting it with rally equipment to run the Golden Eagle's Sports Club Annual Rally which was held the last weekend of August just in time for the first of school. We looked at each other, and as I frowned, Tiffany shrugged her shoulders. "So what," she said. She held up her ring and smiled. We got out and went up the steps and I opened the door for Tiffany.

Tiffany entered the living room first. Bill, his new girlfriend, Georgia Atterbury, and Tiffany's mother were sitting and visiting when we entered the room. Bill stood, Georgia gave a small smile to Tiffany, but sniffed and acted like she was bored.

"I came by to show you the winning car in the rally coming up," Bill said haughtily. "This is what you are missing."

Georgia's face immediately became a frown, and Bill patted her shoulder. "Oh, by the way, Georgia and I are engaged. Show her the rock, honey."

Georgia held out her hand as if she were royalty and expected someone to kiss it. Sure enough, it was a 2 carat solitaire diamond. Her expression of pure pride was all over her face. She thought she had one-upped Tiffany, because she was concerned she was Bill's second choice. She waved her hand around and put it right under Tiffany's nose. I said to myself, "This is gonna be good."

Tiffany looked at it for a moment and smiled so sweetly as only women can do when they know they have the upper hand. Her mother was looking like she felt sorry for her daughter. I was holding Tiffany's left hand. She smiled at Bill and Georgia for a moment creating a very dramatic pause.

"Georgia, honey, that <u>is</u> a pretty little ring," purred Tiffany.

"Little?" said Bill and Georgia in unison as if they could not believe Tiffany was in her right mind.

"Why, yes," Tiffany answered. She pulled her hand from mine and held up her hand with the sparkling diamond ring facing out. "My boyfriend gave me a THREE carat diamond!"

Bill looked like he had been slapped. Georgia's eyes were barely in their sockets, and

Tiffany's mother came, looked, and then had to sit down. Tiffany put her hand right under Georgia's nose like she had done to her. "Now that's a rock, honey," said Tiffany in a smug tone of voice as she tossed her head side to side.

"But, how?" Georgia whispered, with all the attitude gone. She looked at Tiffany, and then everybody turned and looked at me awaiting my answer.

"Tiffany did try on the 2 carat, but the 3 carat looked SO much better," I explained.

Bill shouted, "I DON'T CARE ABOUT THAT! HOW DO YOU EXPECT TO PAY FOR IT?"

"It is already paid for, Bill, old buddy. I paid cash for it."

Bill's head recoiled at the news as if I really had slapped him. His face was red and he was starting to stutter. "B-b-b but how can YOU afford a ring like that?" he stammered. Again, everybody turned to look at me.

"I had some money in savings," I said which was the truth. "And so I transferred some over to my checking account, and gave Mr. Bullock a check. It was no big deal. I have plenty left." I continued.

"Not much left, I'll bet," smirked Bill. All the heads turned toward Bill.

"Oh, I don't know," I began, and all the heads turned to look at me.

"Let's just say that I have more in the bank in MY name than you probably have in the bank in YOUR name instead of your daddy's," I said looking Bill directly in the eye for he knew what I meant. And all the heads turned toward Bill.

He lowered his eyes and I knew the point was well taken. Then, as if gathering some hidden resolve, he squared his shoulders and said, "I saw where you have entered the rally. I have a new Jag with an onboard calculator and all sorts of time distance monitors. I will beat you and your GTO soooo bad." All heads turned to me.

"You know, Bill," I said smiling. "Everything I have I worked for myself. My Daddy didn't give me anything except the will to win. A rally is not a race. It is a time and distance exercise. It requires a very disciplined driver and a good copilot." I took Tiffany's hand and happened to hold up her ring hand. "I have both. Loser has to wax the other's car, fair enough?" All heads turned to Bill.

"Fair enough!" he said angrily. He almost pulled Georgia's arm off as he yanked her up from the couch, and stomped toward the door. "I will win. You will see!" he shouted over his shoulder. He slammed the door on his way out. I heard him slam Georgia's door. I heard him slam HIS door, and he raced the engine as it started. He let out the clutch on the Jag too fast and the car stalled. He started it again and squealed the tires as he left with all heads turned toward the door and laughing.

For the next few minutes everyone crowded around with her dad shaking my hand and slapping me on the back. Her mother even hugged me. She got out the cake she had baked and we enjoyed a great get-to-know-you few minutes before I mentioned to Tiffany we had been on our way to eat. I invited her mother and dad, and we all went to the Palace Hotel Restaurant.

As we ate huge steaks and shared a bottle of champagne, there were people that knew the family and kept coming over to see Tiffany's ring. The word was all over town about the biggest ring most of them had ever seen. Tiffany and her mother could not stop smiling, and seeing her like that almost made me cry.

Later, after dropping off Tiffany and her family, I drove home slowly and pulled into the driveway. I turned off the engine and lights and just sat, trying to adjust to the fact of what had just happened.

Until we could get a house and get married, the only thing I could think of that I wanted to buy myself was a Corvette. I had wanted one for years, but thinking they were too much, I never bought one. Now, I thought humbly, I could afford one.

The next day was a Friday and I didn't have but one class. I called Tiffany at 8:00 am. and told her I was cutting class and wanted her to go with me to pick out something. She didn't really let it sink in until I pulled onto the Chevrolet dealer's new car lot.

"What are you going to do?" she asked smiling.

"Well," I answered. "You got what you want, you already have a new car, and I need something to drive in the Rally. I don't want to trade in the Goat yet, and I thought I would look around."

"Are you going to buy a Corvette?" she asked smugly.

"If they will deal," I smiled.

Because I had been on the lot several times before, the dealership sent their newest sales person out to get a little experience. They actually had three new Corvettes. Two were parked up by the front door and one was on the showroom floor where it was roped off so no one could touch it. There was a white coupe and a blue convertible outside, but on the showroom floor there was the only object in the world that could make me as excited as Tiffany in a swim suit...a shiny, red Corvette convertible with a black top. This was no ordinary 'Vette. It had a 427 cubic inch engine with 3 carburetors and a 4 speed. It was one of the fastest cars ever built in America up until that time. It was nearly as expensive as Tiffany's ring.

I was very polite to Donald Malone, the young man they sent out. I told him I wanted to look at the Corvettes. He took me directly to the stripped down, automatic equipped white coupe first. I listened to the sales pitch, and we looked at the blue convertible as an upgrade.

"Is that one still for sale?" I asked and pointed towards the showroom.

"Yes, of course, but that one is special and is a lot more money."

I countered with, "Let's go look, shall we?" I grabbed Tiffany's hand and squeezed it because of course she was in on the joke.

We entered the showroom, and although a couple of guys waved because they had seen me before, they kept reading the paper with their feet on the desk.

The sales person was obviously out of his comfort zone faced with selling a special high performance auto, and seemed a little awkward for he knew most college kids didn't have much money. He reluctantly lifted the velvet rope for

Tiffany and me and held the car door open for her as I got in under the steering wheel on the driver's side. He was rewarded by a dazzling smile from Tiffany that made him blush.

I ran my hand over the 4-speed shift knob, the dash panel, and touched the steering wheel with almost reverent hands. I turned to the sales person and asked, "What would it take to drive it out of here?"

Donald hesitated knowing that only the owner could make that decision. "Look, Don," he began clearing his throat. "I can't…"

"What if I wrote you a check for it and waited until you called the bank?"

Donald looked at Tiffany to verify he had heard it right. She smiled a little tight-lipped smile and shook her head up and down.

The sales person's whole demeanor suddenly changed. All of a sudden he was calling me mister. Tiffany and I got out and walked to his office. He called the sales manager in, and even he lit up when Donald Malone said, "What kind of a deal for cash can we make today on the Corvette?"

I was given a 500 dollar discount and did not argue because I wanted Donald to make the best commission he was ever going to make. The sales invoice was filled out along with the title application. I handed the sales manager, Ed Thompson, the check, and told him to ask for Mr. Anderson at the bank. I could see him in his glass office as he made the call and the raised eyebrow look for whatever Mr. Anderson had told him.

Ed went and started taking the ropes down from around the Corvette, and the salesmen all came out to see what was going on. They looked at one another as if they could not believe they let a sale on a new Corvette walk through their showroom.

We signed everything, and as we got ready to back the car out, Ed said, "Would you like to hear what the bank president, Mr. Anderson, said?"

"Sure," I responded.

"He said not only was your check good, but give you anything you wanted."

"Cool," I said. "What about mats and a sunvisor mounted Kleenex box?"

"Fair enough," he said. He was back with the mats and the Kleenex box by the time I started the car and let it idle to warm up that big rumbling 427. The big glass door slid to the side and Tiffany and I eased out of the showroom. I stopped and rolled up the windows on the Goat and locked the doors. I got back in and we went for a drive.

For people that do not have a love for cars, and they are only another way to show off their money, or at best a car is just transportation, one could never understand the pent up shout I was feeling as I drove through town with the top down. Corvettes are interesting in themselves, but a new, 1970, shiny red Corvette with the 427 engine letters on the hood, stopped traffic.

We drove out of town toward the curvy road around the lake. Even I was impressed as we went around the curves as if we were on rails. My first little bursts of the throttle were greeted with squeals from Tiffany as the tires left two twin tracks of rubber. To this day, I can still remember how I felt.

Reluctantly, I let Tiffany drive it back to my duplex apartment and I drove the Goat home behind her. At a traffic light, two rednecks in a new Dodge Charger pulled up beside her and started talking trash, and I saw her small smile as she raced the engine a couple of times, and as the light changed, left about 30 feet of smoking rubber. The two guys stared with open mouths and then just turned the corner. They didn't want any of that. I knew I had picked the right girl to marry.

Chapter Fourteen

With only a couple of weeks to prepare for the Golden Eagle Sports Car Club Rally, Tiffany and I practiced every day. We would start at the football stadium and put down in the rally notation every conceivable way we could find to go about 30 miles in every direction. We were told on the instructions sheet the rally would take place at night and would take about 2 hours to run. I figured that meant an hour out and an hour back and even with open roads the rally was to be run close to town and no further out than 30 miles.

In a rally such as this, the instruction sheet tells one how to drive a route using a notation of

"T's" and notes and the miles per hour between check points or stages. This particular rally also included fill in the blanks about signs, businesses, etc. and these were to be added to the driving scores to determine first place. There was to be 3 top place finishes with little plaques and gifts all the way to two hundred dollars and a trophy for first place.

Tiffany proved to be a fast learner, but knowing she could also drive well I decided to be the navigator and let her drive. This was a long time before computers as we know them, but on the huge IBM computer at school, my friend, John Smith (real name), who was also a brilliant engineering student, printed out time distance charts so that we could use 2 stop watches and a slide rule and know just how fast and for how long we needed to drive between check points.

As there is no practice time allowed on the rally stages, the driver cannot drive the route by memory. The main job of the co-driver, or navigator, is to tell the driver about the course as the team is racing through it. He/she is also responsible for ensuring the team arrives at each point of the rally at their designated time to avoid time penalties: one minute late or one minute early can mean the difference between winning and losing. The driver and co-driver must trust each other and truly work as a team. Tiffany and I could do that. I smiled to myself just thinking of Bill and Georgia arguing on which way to go.

The rally was to begin exactly at 7:00 p.m. with each car leaving in 30 second intervals. We drew for starting times and we were third car out behind my math professor, Dr. Smith and his 2 year old Jag XKE, and another teacher in a new Camaro SS I didn't know. Bill and Georgia were number 8 out of 20 cars.

As we got in line about 6:30, the new Corvette drew a crowd especially with Tiffany driving. She had her hair in a pony tail, and had on white short shorts and a red, sleeveless blouse. She wore a white tennis visor cap with her hair sticking through the back of the cap. She looked beautiful as always. Several of my friends commented how hard it was going to be for me to focus on the race and not her. No problem, I was somewhat used to her, and she was focused enough for both of us.

Bill sat in his car staring at us until Georgia took her hand and turned his head around. It was going to be a long night for them. Bill was driving and Georgia was the navigator.

At 6:45 everyone was handed a packet of instructions by a member of the sports car club. As soon as I saw the instructions, I knew we were set. It matched a couple of the routes we had mapped.

I had put the top up on the Corvette to cut down on wind and exhaust noise, and at 6:55 the starter yelled, "PEOPLE, START YOUR ENGINES!" He looked at Tiffany and me and lowered his voice, "I always love saying that."

The number two car was a nice looking yellow Camaro SS-396 with fairly loud glasspack mufflers, but nothing to compare when Tiffany roared the 427 to life through the outside exhaust pipes. It was not loud like a drag car, but a low pitched moan that meant it was all business. The left front fender would rise a little every time Tiffany raced the throttle from the tremendous torque of the engine.

At exactly 7:00 the starter counted it down from 5 to the word, "Go!" and Dr. Smith chirped the tires a little as he left. Even though this was not a real race you had to drive a certain speed for a defined length of time. So, there was a little need to accelerate to speed. The first command was to drive 45 mph for 6 blocks and turn right at the corner.

The Camaro left a little more rubber. But, everyone smiled and cheered as Tiffany hit the accelerator hard enough to leave rubber AND smoke for about 10 feet.

"Easy," I laughed. "Drive to 48, count two and cut back to 45 until we get to the corner. Brake hard but don't slide around the corner. Stay at 45 for one mile and at the sign for Tennessee State Highway 70 turn left. From there for 3 miles stay at 60. The next turn is an on ramp to the left. It looks like 15 miles will be at 70 on the Interstate. Cool!"

"At 15 miles out there will be an exit ramp. The name on the sign is our first fill in the blank. That's easy. That exit is for Crossville. Now, here is where our training pays off. There are a lot of turns right and left on unfamiliar streets in Crossville and the first check point is just as we get ready to come back toward town."

As we drove through town and out on the highway I made an observation. There are no ugly girls in a Corvette. The fact there was one going by in a 427 Corvette with a girl, already gorgeous, driving made the growling red Corvette a point and look proposition for everyone we met.

Tiffany was concentrating with a slight, grim smile on her face as she smoothly went through the gears. No time for small talk, but once we hit the Interstate and she was at speed I patted her hand resting on the gear shift knob. She squeezed my hand and smiled at me. She knew we were doing well.

In Crossville, even my understanding of the notation was put to the test as we turned from paved roads to dirt roads. Going left one time and right the next and circling back it was going to be easy to get confused. Tiffany never hesitated. She trusted my instructions and I trusted her driving. After about 20 minutes we saw the first check point. We slid a little as we stopped. The timer said we were 7 seconds ahead of where we needed to be. As we waited for our time to leave, I told Tiffany to drive at 68 for 5 seconds, and then do 70, as we got on the Interstate back home.

As we got to the Cookeville exit, our rally route left the freeway about 2 miles from town onto a two lane asphalt highway and then turned off on a dirt road for a mile, then left onto another paved road. We were to travel for 2 minutes at 50 and then turn left again. The second stage check point was out in the country. We were 5 seconds <u>behind</u> this time, but I knew it was because we were being careful. Making <u>up</u> time was easy in the Corvette.

Tiffany drove as she was told, and we filled in the blanks for Burma Shave signs and the names of small towns like Tic, and Fer Tic. Same town actually, but was named twice because it was split in two and on different sides of the creek. I love Tennessee. Look it up. It is on the map by Gainesboro.

Coming back through the countryside, we met Bill and Georgia who waved and stopped us to see where the check point was. Georgia was in tears because Bill blamed her for being lost when it was really him that would not follow her directions. Quickly we told them where they went wrong, and a little fast driving they would be in good shape for the end of the Rally. We looked at one another and smiled as they sped away.

We got back to the stadium and as the timer from the Sports Car Club clicked the watch he told me we had tied with Dr. Smith at 3 seconds off and the fill in the blanks were going to be the difference.

We sat and watched the others returning. We knew they should have been exactly 30 seconds apart. Some were way late and no one was early. Bill actually came in within just a few seconds late. It was close enough to make me look again at our fill in the blanks. We had them all.

After 30 minutes everyone was in and we went to one of the classrooms in the corner of the stadium to see the results. Bill was number 3 on time distance, and we waited for the judges to tell us who won. Finally, the head judge stepped up to the mike on the podium.

"People, this is the closest rally we have ever had. Car number one and car number three tied on the time distance part. However, drum roll please, car number 3 got ALL the blanks right and number one missed two!" He lifted up the trophy and the check and said loudly, "Tiffany and Don are the winners!"

It was bedlam. We were patted on the back and Tiffany bounced up and down with her pony-tail waving as we hugged and I got a little kiss.

Afterward, Dr. Smith asked to see our computer or calculator we had used. He could not believe two stop watches, a slide rule, and a printed chart had beaten his custom setup. He said he was going to tell every class about us.

Bill came up and surprisingly offered his hand and said, "If we had to get beat, I am glad it was you guys."

Georgia and Tiffany hugged and we all went to the Palace Hotel restaurant for coffee and dessert. I was going to let him off the hook about washing and waxing the car, but not Tiffany.

"No way," she said firmly. "Come by Don's about 10 a.m. tomorrow and you can clean off the dust and bugs from the Rally and give it a good waxing!"

He may not have liked it, but he knew when Tiffany meant business. Sure enough, he was there the next morning with Georgia, sponges, rags and a bucket. We all helped, laughing and spraying one another and the girls buffed out the wax after Bill and I rubbed it on. We even joined in and washed and waxed Bill's Jag. I don't hold a grudge, and he knew he had been bested. His dad was a lawyer in Nashville with a lot of rich friends, and he knew he was going places. I didn't know yet if I could trust him, but we were friends because he knew he could trust <u>me</u>.

I entered my Senior year in pre-law at Tennessee Tech in the fall of 1970. I had taken the time to get Mr. Davis's suggestions for my electives and found out Bill, Georgia, Tiffany, and me were in 3 classes together. It was going to be a busy but fun year.

Tennessee Tech's football team had a running back by the name of Larry Shrieber, and a linebacker named Jim Youngblood. Both were destined to play for the pros. The cannons were loud and often that year.

A few days after school started, Tiffany's mother asked had we set a date yet to get married? We looked at each other and realized we had been so busy we had not even thought about it. Okay, maybe Tiffany had, but it was not something that had even crossed my mind. I told Tiffany to pick the date. We had the money, and all we had to do was set a date around school. She thought we could have it ready by Thanksgiving weekend. I said, "What? No Justice of the Peace?"

"You are really cutting into your sugar, you know that?" and she punched me on the arm.

I put a few thousand into a joint account, and Tiffany was actually pretty frugal. She nixed for the Pope to do the wedding, and the 100,000 white doves were replaced with small packages of bird seed for people to throw instead of rice. The Corvette would just have to do to drive away after the wedding I said and she agreed. No carriage and horses for <u>me</u>.

Chapter Fifteen

The wedding was set for the day before Thanksgiving at First Baptist Church in Cookeville. My mother and dad were called and I told them to drive over from Arkansas the week before for us to spend some time together. They were flabbergasted to hear how well I was doing. Both were going to fall in love, I knew, with Tiffany and her family.

One thing I had overlooked that was pointed out by Nellie and Mr. Mingus, where were we going to live? My little duplex was probably uncool, I was told, for Tiffany. So, we drove around for a couple of days looking at houses.

I still had never told Tiffany how much money I had in the bank. When I told her she could spend for house and furnishings up to a couple hundred thousand she almost went into shock. In 1970 that was a LOT of money.

Mr. Davis came through with an even better solution. He lived on a 20 acre estate on a hill overlooking Cookeville, and he had just built a new huge home to sell with a 4 car garage, swimming pool, tennis court, and beautiful trees and lawn on another 10 acres across the road from him. For a wedding present, he offered it to us for free! He made us promise to invite him for supper once in a while. For that house he could have moved in!

He gave me the deed in a little ceremony at his estate, and Tiffany, Georgia, Nellie and Tiffany's mom had a blast decorating it. My only input was the library/office. I wanted an old round top Wurlitzer record player full of old 45's. They were cheap in 1970. I had to have a big mahogany desk like Mr. Davis's. I also had a good sized table and all leather chairs and a couch. It had a fireplace and I loved opening the French doors and sitting looking out over the pool with Tiffany. Somehow, getting much studying done was always after she had gone home. I stayed there the last month before the wedding, and Tiffany and her entourage came and went every day moving in furniture and accessories to get it all just right.

My mother and dad drove over on Wednesday before the wedding and found the house from my directions and by asking a few people. They were amazed everyone they asked knew where I lived.

My dad and I had not seen eye to eye before I left home. He was very controlling. I took it because I loved him, but I still left home to be on my own. I realize now he only wanted the best for me. My set of values are his best gift to me.

Mom and Dad had called when they got to town, and Tiffany and her mother came and waited with me. I watched as my folks drove up in their new Pontiac Grand Prix and got out. My dad kept looking at the directions written on a piece of paper to see if he had them right. I opened the door while they were still standing in the circular driveway in front of the house. Tiffany and I went on out and went through the teary eyed hugging and greeting thing while Mrs. Parker stood and watched from the doorway dabbing at her eyes with a handkerchief. My mother hugged Tiffany, and so did my dad when I introduced her.

Whatever real or imagined which was between my dad and me was gone. I was happy to be accepted as a man of my own by my dad.

We all walked arm and arm into the house and Tiffany introduced her mother at the door. Tiffany and her mother were old friends instantly with my mother, and they whisked her off to see the house and I was left alone with my dad. I showed him my huge office, the pool, and we walked into the garage. He had heard about the cars, and his eyes really lit up when I gave him the keys to the Corvette. He started the engine and smiled, listening to the rumble as he revved the engine a little.

"Let's go for a drive, Pop. They won't even know we are gone for a while."

He did not need to be asked twice. He slowly backed the car out of the garage, put it in gear and drove around the house, up the drive-way to the entrance, and as he turned onto the road he just could not resist giving it a little gas and pinned us to the seat.

"Man oh man, son! What a car!" We looked at the speedometer and we were doing over 85 in less than a quarter of a mile. He made a face and slowed to 60 as we drove through a couple of curves. He looked like I must have when I first got the car, as he drove expertly around the curves, and he would open it up a little on the straights. We both were enjoying the ride.

After about an hour, we both agreed we might have to go back. As we rode along at 45 my dad apologized to me for not letting me buy the old Ford. He had not understood at the time it was the car, not the prideful aura of a hot rod, that had made me want that particular car. He too loved cars, especially the old ones, but he had never had the time or the money to build them making a living for the family.

"You know, Dad," I spoke quietly. "If you and mom will move back, I will buy you a nice house out here by us and we can buy or build a garage in town to build hot rods. Fast Eddie's Speed Shop is for sale. Not only does he have a nice inventory, but he has a spacious 4 bay shop and 2 lifts. He already has the best mechanics in town, and a good clientele. Let me buy it and us be partners. It would be lots of fun. You would only work on what you wanted to and we will even hire college kids to sell speed parts. We could build our own cars while having a business building for others."

"You know, I have been thinking along those lines too. Street rodding is really taking off.

The cars are mostly being built in California, but we could advertise and have a very nice market right here."

"Let me ask Mom if she would move back. She really didn't want to leave before, so, I am sure she would consider it."

We put up the car, and, as soon as we got in the house, Mom grabbed Dad and drug him off to show him everything. He looked over her head and smiled at me as he went. Tiffany came up and took my hand beaming from the visit with my mother.

"Oh, Don, I love your mom. Do you think they might want to move back?"

"They might," I said quietly.

Chapter Sixteen

The wedding was really something for Cookeville. Mr. Davis was my best man, and Mrs. Parker was Tiffany's Maid of Honor. Bill, Georgia, and two more couples made up of friends were also in the wedding. The reception was in the ballroom of the Palace Hotel. I only got to dance a couple of times with Tiffany, because every man there wanted to dance with such a gorgeous creature. I did get the last one, however, and that was the best one.

Tiffany's mother and mine promised to load up all the presents and take them to the house. My mom and dad were staying another week at the house while we were gone, my dad had quit his job at the dealership where he worked, and they were making plans to move to Cookeville. We had found them a nice house just a mile or so from ours and they were to close on it while we were gone.

My wedding night was in the bridal suite of the Palace Hotel. When we opened the door to our room it was filled with balloons and there were rose petals on the bed. There was even a bottle of champagne, but it never got opened.

The next morning, not early, Tiffany and I drove to Gatlinburg for 5 days. We had a blast driving the 'Vette through the East Tennessee countryside and the Blue Ridge Mountains. With "Just Married" written all over the car, we got lots of thumb ups and honks as we drove to the motel, which was situated on a small, rushing creek.

My honeymoon to the most beautiful girl in the world was all I had imagined it would be. We went out to downtown Gatlinburg every night. We watched as they made stick candy and gave us free pieces to taste. There was a place that had man made snow for skiing where I found out I needed a lot of practice to compete in that sport.

We ate great every night, even sampling pizza for the first time. In 1970 pizza was fairly new to small towns, but we all knew it was going to sweep the fast food business. I made a mental note to see if Mr. Davis was open to the idea of partnering a Pizza Hut franchise in Cookeville.

At breakfast the day we were leaving to go back to Cookeville, I thought I saw Wendell Dixon of all people in the motel restaurant. For once he was sitting alone. Even his friends did not come near him unless he had made a score and could buy drinks and entertainment for them. Sure enough, as we walked outside he approached me.

"You tell your boss I ain't forgettin' what he did. He beat me out of a lot of money."

"You know, Dixon. You got what you deserved. You would have beat a little old lady out of a fortune just for greed. If you had been a little less greedy you might <u>could</u> have bought that land from her, and both of you made some money."

He started to take a step toward me, but when he saw the look on my face, he stopped and reminded himself he was alone.

"Besides," I spoke between clenched teeth. "Mr. Richard Davis does not need bodyguards like you to protect him. He won't spook and he won't run. He will kick your butt in a standup fight, and he has enough friends that we will run you and your goons out of town if you show your face in Cookeville."

"You just tell him to watch his back."

"He will, and I will help watch it too. You are a coward, and we know what we are up against. For your information, <u>you</u> are being watched already. So, you better be pretty sneaky when you come for him."

Actually, I thought that was a lie, but the look on his face was rewarding, because he wasn't sure but that I was telling the truth. I was going to make it true when I got back and could talk to Richard.

Tiffany and I didn't talk much as we drove home through the countryside. There were still enough trees with leaves to make it a beautiful trip. All the hardwood trees in that part of the state have gorgeous bright red, orange, and yellow colors in the Fall. It had been everything I had ever wanted for my honeymoon weekend except for the run in with Dixon. Tiffany put her head on my shoulder and was quiet for she knew what was going on. I knew I could count on her. Southern women stand by their men. (That ought to be a song.)

The next day, I went to see Richard. He was on the phone, but motioned for me to come on in. He hung up quickly when he saw how serious I was.

"Don't tell me a gorgeous woman like Tiffany made you sad," he said smiling a big lecherous grin.

I smiled too. "You know better than that, but something happened I think you need to know."

I told him everything that had happened including the part about telling Dixon he was being watched.

He looked around his office as if to assure himself we were alone and, lowering his voice and bending his head close, he said, "You know, Don, I have never been married. You are as close to being a son as anyone I have ever known, and I know I can trust you. I have already heard that Dixon has been shooting off his mouth. The truth is I DO have someone shadowing him. For now, there is no need for you to know all about who, but let me assure you Dixon and his goons would not stand a chance."

He smiled at me for I was obviously relieved. He patted my shoulder, and he said, "Now let's go eat a steak. I am starved. How about you?"

I was hungry too. I had not eaten since the day before after everything happened. We walked over to the Palace Hotel after I called Tiffany to meet us. Every eye in the place watched as she came in and kissed me on the mouth, Richard on the cheek, and hugged us both. Tiffany's ring put rainbows all around her and our table as we ate. There were still women coming up to see her ring. I was a lot happier knowing Richard knew.

Chapter Seventeen

The next day, my mom, Tiffany's mom, and Nellie offered to cook for all of us. We invited Richard, of course, and we had a great supper of smothered pork chops, mashed potatoes, home made rolls, and all the trimmings. I got a moment alone with Tiffany and said, "You know, I still don't know if you can cook."

She smiled and said, "I made the salad and the tea."

"Oh," was all I said.

She hit me on the arm and smiled sweetly, "We got a can opener as a wedding gift. You won't starve."

"It is a good thing I moved my mom over here close to us, huh?"

I got hit again as she handed me a bowl of green beans and said, "The honeymoon is over, and so now make yourself useful!"

At my frown, I did get a kiss big enough to take my breath away and a smile. "It is not ALL the way over is it?" I asked, turning my lower lip down in a pout.

"Maybe not ALL the way," she smiled and winked. I was ready for everyone to go home right that moment.

Later, while the women cleared the table and did the dishes, the men went outside to talk and smoke by the patio fireplace as men have done since cave man times. No one even dared to ask could they smoke inside in my and Tiffany's new home. Richard, my dad, Mr. Parker, and

Thurber all took one of Richard's huge imported cigars and lit up while we talked. I told them that I was not grown up enough for one of those yet which got a big laugh. The talk was mostly small about the Tech football team, the weather, helping my dad move in when the moving van got there on Thursday, and finally, it grew quite as we stared into the fire and savored the moment.

"Men," said Richard breaking the silence. We all watched as he knocked off an inch of ashes into the fire. He continued, "Don here told me about eating pizza in Gatlinburg last weekend, and that maybe we ought to consider investing in fast food franchises. After checking it out, Pizza Hut, Burger King, and a company called McDonald's are really offering some start up help if we want to invest a little. I would be willing to put up half of any franchise any of you want to invest in.

Mr. Wayne and Don have already made an offer on Fast Eddie Cantor's business, and Don and I would like to have a Pizza Hut franchise. McDonald's is big and so is Burger King. What do you men think?"

Thurber Mingus asked, "Who is going to work in them? Nellie and me are a little old to go to work now."

"That is the best part," countered Richard. "We are sitting in a college town that is an hour and a half from Nashville one way and Knoxville the other way. So, we have a willing work force, and a ready market waiting for us to open the doors. We just go by and take the money to the bank. I bet you and Nellie can do that, Thurber." The slight smile from Thurber meant he was with us.

"You know, men," spoke up Mr. Parker. "All y'all have money. I have a little in savings, but not a tremendous amount. I am not sure I can afford it."

At that Richard Davis laughed out loud. "Hey, don't forget. Your daughter just married into money." After another round of laughter subsided, Richard spoke softly, "Put in what you have that you can afford, I will loan you the rest at very, very good terms. You can even pay me back out of earnings. Now, do you want a Burger King or a McDonald's?"

As it turned out, Thurber found out that Captain D's was being bought out by Long John Silver's Corporation from Kentucky. So, he and Nellie bought the local Captain D's and opened a Long John Silver's. Dad and I opened Wayne's Speed And Rod Building Shop. Richard and I opened the first Pizza Hut in Cookeville, a Burger King, and I went halves with Mr. and Mrs. Parker on a McDonald's across the street from Tennessee Tech on one of Mrs. Gentry's properties she didn't know she owned. Within a year the Parkers paid off their small loans and bought property from Nellie and built a very big and flourishing McDonald's franchise of their own along the interstate and Sparta highway.

Within two years everyone was doing very well. Mr. and Mrs. Parker bought 5 acres from Richard and built their dream house and furnished it like they had always wanted. My dad and I built several rods for people including a '40 Ford Coupe for Tiffany and me. Mom and Dad built a beautiful 1934 Ford two door sedan. Both cars were powered by chromed Chevrolet engines and won awards in the Nashville Hot Rod Shows and were in several rod magazines. Friday nights we all went to Nellie and Thurber's Long John Silver's for fish and fries. Richard joined us if he could.

Tiffany, Georgia, Bill, and I all graduated Class Of 1972. I was Bill's best man and Tiffany was Georgia's Maid of Honor that June. Tiffany got a job teaching at the Elementary school in Cookeville. Georgia decided to stay at home, and Bill and I entered the law school at Vanderbilt University in Nashville. We both graduated with honors and passed our bar exams. Although we were as competitive with one another about as much as we could be, we actually became good friends. I had all my classes on two days a week, and I even stayed with them at their mansion one night a week while I went to law school. I commuted to school and one night a week is all I had to stay from home. We made it fine and there were always good homecomings for Tiffany and me, but it was still great to not have to be away from each other for even one night after the year ended.

Bill became a defensive trial lawyer and I was an assistant prosecuting attorney in Cookeville under Richard Davis. My office was just down the hall from his, and under his mentoring I learned when to temper justice and when to put the bad guys away. In 1975 Richard ran for State Senator from Cookeville and won in a landslide. That year I was appointed Prosecuting Attorney for Putnam County in his place.

The fast food franchises made everybody all the money we would ever need. Richard and I bought several franchises for Pizza Hut including one on the interstate and one by the college which offered delivery. We bought one in Crossville and one in Lebanon, with both having easy Interstate 40 access. Tiffany and I bought one of our own in Sparta and once in while we would pick up a pizza and go parking at Lookout Point and eat pizza and make out a little.

Mr. and Mrs. Parker did very well with the McDonald's franchises and I helped them form a corporation for all their franchises. They soon had them all over Tennessee and even in a few bordering states as well.

Nellie and Thurber Mingus did well with Long John Silver's also. As the new corporation grew, Nellie and Thurber, having money, grew along with it, and eventually had 22 profitable locations in several states. Thurber finally admitted he LOVED going to the bank.

Chapter Eighteen

Tiffany suggested we start going to church. So, we began going to the First Assembly of God which is a local Pentecostal church. I confess, for someone raised in a Baptist church, the services were a little different. I was of the opinion God had already blessed me way beyond measure. It wasn't that I did not need God, but I went through lip service in my praise of Him. When you have everything what more could one ask for?

I came home from work one day in October of 1978 and Tiffany had cooked a great meal with steak and all the trimmings. She was humming to herself as she worked with a small smile on her face.

"You seem to be in a good mood," I smiled.

"Yes, I am. I went to the doctor today and it was a good report."

She had my full attention now. "I didn't know you were sick. Although I have noticed you having a little nausea in the morning."

She sat down at the table beside me and took my hands in hers and said quietly,"What would you say if I told you we were going to have a baby?"

My shocked look made her smile as I stuttered, "I, I thought you were on the pill."

"Oh, I quit taking them a couple of months ago."

"You could have let me in on it," I said. I was a little surprised and somewhat irritated we had not talked about it.

"I did. That is why I am pregnant, lover."

We both laughed, and I really did not care. I was ready to have kids. My parents and Tiffany's parents were already starting to ask when we were going to bless them with grandkids.

I let Tiffany and two grandmothers do most of the shopping and planning for a baby. We bought baby furniture and clothes and made the room across from ours the baby's first room. Tiffany and I painted it a light blue for I joked about sending it back if it was not a boy. I could not imagine a little girl to raise.

I have no idea why babies always come at night. June 10th around 2 a.m. Tiffany just put her hand on my shoulder and said, "Don, it is time to go."

I was awake instantly out of a dead sleep, and hastily put on jeans and a sweatshirt while I grabbed the two small suit cases we had already packed. I helped Tiffany get dressed and ran for the garage. The GTO was the closest and I hit the button for the garage door opener as I fumbled for the keys. I squealed the tires a little as I backed out and drove around to pick up Tiffany. She had called the hospital, and our parents were right behind us as we pulled into the hospital parking lot.

I went with Tiffany into the birthing room to hold her hand. Big mistake. She had a big contraction and squeezed my hand so hard it almost brought me to my knees. I was praying and crying, but soon we had a red, wrinkled little son. We named him Richard Don Wayne. Weren't we clever? However, to this day he is still called Ricky Don by everyone. They handed him to me in a towel and a blanket and I sat and held him for over an hour while they attended to Tiffany.

I counted his fingers and toes and pulled back the blanket to let our parents look. He had very little light colored hair and his eyes were so tightly shut I still could not tell what color his eyes were. He was beautiful.

After the birth of my son, my life changed completely. I changed his diapers for the first couple of weeks because Tiffany found she had a weak stomach. I would hold him until I was ready to walk out the door to go to work and I picked him up as soon as I came home. It is a miracle he ever learned to walk.

By the time he was two years old, I had a playpen filled with toys in a corner of my office for when Tiffany and Ricky Don came to visit. We would take the GTO at first, but soon we bought a new Chevy van with custom wheels to take the load of luggage which accompanies a baby whenever we went out. I kept the GTO and the Corvette. I just could not part with my childhood I suppose.

We still went out of course, baby and all. However, with two sets of grandparents so close, we had willing and able sitters whenever Tiffany and I wanted to go out just the two of us. The first time or two we would run back and forth to the phone checking on him. I loved being a dad and so when Tiffany said she was going to have another baby I was happy. The second time I wanted a girl.

Ricky Don had just turned three when Suzy Leigh was born. She had light blond hair and blue eyes just like her mother. The first time I held her and she held my finger in her little hand, I was hooked. I loved her too.

I had been feeling guilty that I might not could love another child as much as I did my son, but now I know how God can say He loves each of us in a special way. I was going to learn just how special Suzy Leigh was going to be.

Chapter Nineteen

After only a few days at home the doctor called and asked us to come to his office. He was very somber as he told us that our baby girl was born with a form of polio, and might not ever be able to walk correctly. I just stared at him. After all the blessings God had given me in my life, why would we be given this? What had I done wrong? I went to church and my tithe money alone had built two churches in Cookeville already. We said Grace over every meal, and I prayed every morning over the day's business. What more did I need to do?

This form of polio is a birth defect that occurs in from 10,000 to 20,000 births a year. There are three main classes and luckily Susie had the "occulta" diagnosis which meant we would have to wait and see. Most people live a normal life and a few have to use a cane or crutches in some cases.

After a few months I was encouraged Susie could sit up even though she looked a little bent over. Holding that baby in my arms made me start to learn to pray.

My dad was a deacon in a Baptist church when I was living at home. I had heard all the sermons about trusting and believing, but I am not sure I had a personal relationship with God and Jesus. I carried my Bible back and forth to church like a good Baptist kid so that on Sunday morning I could make a 100 per cent on my offering envelope in Sunday School class. It never occurred to me to smoke or drink, I didn't curse, and I was several years away from having sex. In short, I was the "squarest" kid I knew. My nickname was "sister" because I was assumed to be so pious. It was not derisive, I was just a good kid. I played football and baseball, I was in the church choir and the school glee club, I had the male lead in the Junior and Senior plays, and I liked everybody. When pushed, I fought back well enough no one messed with me. I was an ordinary, small town young man. So, why was my baby sick?

I had to search a little to find the Bible my mother sent me in Viet Nam for one of my birthdays. It was packed away with old high school annuals and a tour book or two from the Navy. I dusted it off, reread my parents' words of encouragement in the flyleaf, and not knowing where to start, I started in Genesis, the first book.

I read about God creating the universe and man, becoming disappointed, and if it had not been for Noah, would have destroyed them all. I read about Joseph, who was sold into slavery by his jealous brothers, but through him God brought the children of Abraham to Egypt to be taken care of through a devastating famine. They prospered so well the Egyptians enslaved them. When they cried out to God he used Moses to lead them out and took care of them until they entered the promised land. All through the Old Testament God took care of His people, delivered and healed them. Why not my baby?

It was not until I got to the New Testament and started reading about Jesus that my faith started to awaken and grow. I read about Him healing the blind, the ones that could not walk, lepers, and He even brought Lazarus back from the dead! Now we were getting somewhere! So, what did I need to do to have Him heal my little girl? What was the "formula" for receiving from God? I kept reading my Bible and praying but I did not see any results. Finally, I went and called my dad. I asked him to walk over and we would go for a ride out to the lake.

I backed out the Corvette, sprayed a little water on it, and we both were unusually quiet as we wiped it off. We both agreed it still looked like new though by now it was several years old. I lowered and stowed the top and we drove through the countryside and out by the lake. We made small talk as we both enjoyed the Fall leaves in colors that only are in Tennessee in October.

We drove all the way to an outlook that Mr. Mingus brought me to a couple of times. I had to check out his claim when he said that he owned several hundred acres of that hill top. He put in his will that when he died it all came to me and my heirs. I was so hoping my Suzy was going to be one of those heirs.

Dad and I sat down on a large, bare rock and just felt the sunshine on our faces all warm, touched by just a hint of cool from a breeze off the water.

"What's on your mind, son," my dad asked quietly. "You did not bring me all the way out here to see the lake."

"No," I smiled. "I need to ask you something of a spiritual nature."

"Sure, go ahead."

"Dad, how do I get God to heal my baby?"

"Oh, goodness," he exclaimed. "That is a huge question. Man has been asking and searching how to manipulate God since we began to call on Him."

"I know," I began quietly as I watched the little wind waves chase the birds flying low across the lake. "It is just that I can not stand to see my baby ill when I know that God can answer my prayer and heal her."

"You know, son," he said as he turned and looked at me with tears in his eyes. "I can't tell you how or why, but let me give you a testimony. In 1959 there was a virus going around and people were even dying from it called the Asian Flu. You had a high fever for several days and I sat night and day to keep cool, wet wash clothes on your forehead and fed you aspirin. That was all we knew to do."

He shifted position a little, as if embarrassed from such a rare show of emotion. "I really was worried about you," he continued. "You were not getting better, and I did not know what to do.

So, I prayed while you were sleeping. I asked God to do what I could not do. I told Him I loved you just like He loved His son. I had read where Jesus' sacrifice gave us power through faith in His name to have whatever we asked, and healing was one of the "benefits" spoken of in Psalms 103. I had my hands clasped and my elbows on the edge of your bed with my head bowed as I prayed. I was crying softly to not wake you when I felt your hand cover my hands. I could not believe it! You were completely cool to the touch after having fever for several days! I grabbed you and hugged you while I cried and thanked God for giving my boy back to me!"

With tears welling in my own eyes imagining that scene, I watched fascinated as a couple of tears ran down his weathered face to be wiped away by a big hand. He sniffed and smiled and said, "I still cannot recall that without shedding a tear or two."

I put my arm around him and we both sobbed for a moment.

"Dad, it is already three o'clock. Let's pray for Suzy before we head back."

With his arm still around my shoulder, I prayed, "Dear, Jesus, heal my baby. I don't know what to do but just bring her to you and ask in faith. Only you can heal her."

That was it. We didn't shout at that moment or do anything special. I just knew in my heart everything was going to be okay.

The ride back from the lake was not nearly as somber as the ride to the lake. But when we drove into the driveway, there were several cars parked in the circular driveway and my heart dropped that something terrible had happened.

When I left the house Suzy had been tired from playing and wanted to take a nap. I pulled in front of the house and Tiffany, Mother, and Tiffany's mom came out of the door excitedly.

"What is going on?" I almost shouted. "How's Suzy?"

Tiffany got to me first and hugged me so tightly I could hardly breathe.

"Don," she started and then burst into tears. "It is Suzy!"

"What, what?" I was impatient, but almost afraid I did not want to know. Tiffany calmed and started to speak, but at that moment I heard an excited little voice.

"Daddy, watch me!" Suzy shouted. She came out from behind my mother. I was amazed as for the first time in her little life, she jumped from the step and ran to me with arms out-stretched.

"What is going on? Even though she is two years old, I have never seen her run before," I said as I looked at Tiffany.

With her arms still around me and Suzy, she said, "You won't believe this. Around three o'clock she woke from her nap and got out of bed by herself and came running down the hall! We were sitting and talking in the den, and I could not picture who the kid was that could be running down the hall. I almost fainted as Suzy came running into the room and actually jumped up into my arms! She could barely walk before!"

Overcome with emotion, I sank to my knees holding Suzy as I cried. That was exactly the time when Dad and I were praying!

Today Suzy is so beautiful, erect and straight she has even done some modeling. No one believes she once had a form of polio. She is a Sophomore at the University of Tennessee and is a cheerleader. Ricky Don is attending Law School at Vanderbilt University in Nashville.

Thurber Mingus died in 1984 with a will and a set of keys to his round top trunk. He left its contents to me and in it was 200,000 dollars cash and enough bearer bonds and stock certificates in companies like General Motors, Ford and Westinghouse that in today's market, and after splitting thousands of times, we are all multi millionaires. We gave enough money to Tennessee Tech to build the new Richard Davis athletic complex after he passed away in 1991, and all they have to do is keep the cannons, one in each end zone, and fire them off when Tech scores. Some seasons I bet Mr. Davis smiles that boyish smile a lot.

THE END

Other books by Don Horne

Anthem To The Wind
Beginnings/Book 1

The Prodigal
Anthem To The Wind /Book 2

Cannons In The Fall

All are available through Amazon.com or other retailers.

Horne Publishing
302 Cascade Drive
Red Oak, Texas 75154